Index

5

Cinderello

A faerie tale for male feetlovers

111

Appendix

Glass loafers Gallery

Cinderello

A faerie tale for male feetlovers

A note from the author:

This faerie tale is dedicated to all feetlovers. And with that I don't mean only foot lovers, but all feet, shoes, loafers, slippers, executives, socks... and all the variants derived from the foot, that beautiful part of a man's body for which we live and feel.

This story wants to put into words that pursuit that we carry out every day for that loved one. I recommend reading in Spanish to appreciate the difference in illustrations in each of the versions. The illustrations do not fit the description of the text, since I like that the imagination of each reader is free to imagine while enjoying the reading. The images are just a help for the rich imagination that my version of this wonderful and eternal faerie tale has always suggested to me.

*It goes for all of you, dear feetlovers.
I hope you enjoy the text and illustrations as much as I do.*

The Man With Pretty Feet

ay was a man who caused envy, sighs, jealousy and hope. As soon as he saw him, his beauty was not only apparent, but it was also discovered that he had many virtues that made him a desired man. He has always lived in a manor house in the Austrias neighborhood, one of the most charming neighborhoods in the Villa. The entire building was owned by his parents. Until the age of twelve, Jay had a happy life, until his mother died and his father married again, this time to a man, Mr. Dorrel, a graying muscled man in his sixties. With Mr. Dorrel came his two sons, who became his stepbrothers, Crispin and Vachel. After the death of his father when Jay was twenty years old, Jay had no choice but to adapt to new rules of living in that wonderful five-floor house. However, it was already beginning to show signs of lack of maintenance,

and since Jay didn't want everything his father had done to make it the prettiest house in the barrio was for nothing, he spent a lot of time cleaning and decorating it.

However, Crispin and Vachel, along with their father Dorrel, knew very well how to give Jay more work to keep him busy. Thus they prevented him from dedicating himself to studying his career and devoting himself to what he liked the most, which was painting, reading about the classical world and learning languages. After a few more years, they managed to get Jay to dedicate the whole day to cleaning, ordering, sweeping, scrubbing, cooking and doing some pleasant (depending on the point of view) chore that was a little demeaning. And this particular task was to offer his body for the pleasure of his stepbrothers. Once or twice a month or so, Jay was harassed, humiliated, and forced into relationships with this pair of smelly, sweaty men. Dorrel, his stepfather, did not want Jay to serve him in this way, but he was the one who was dedicated to ordering him and inventing the most fanciful practices for poor Jay. The practices did not go beyond offering his mouth and ass for the most animal sex. Over the years Jay got used to this great duty to fulfill if he wanted to stay in that house.

Jay might have enjoyed these chores if basically his stepbrothers had been nice and kind. Crispin was the oldest of the two stepbrothers, however the shortest in height. His head was misshapen and broad, reminiscent of a seedy alien from a double-session black-and-white American movie from the 1950s. In addition, his large eyes helped to remember that resemblance. He had a severe halitosis problem that he did not want to solve since he loved to eat garlic with bread. He was basically "daddy's boy", having everything he wanted at all times, such as a drum kit which he pounded away late at night even when Jay had to get up at five in the morning to make their breakfasts.

Vachel, although he was younger, was the tallest of all. With sallow skin, very tall, around 6'4"height. He might appear corpulent, although he was really well-distributed fat because what he liked most was eating. With cropped hair, a boxer's broad nose, and a pockmarked, scarred face. Unlike his brother, his breath did smell good, although the rest of his body didn't. This was a consequence of his neglect to find a job. He was a specialist in contemplating the ceiling while eating ketchup-flavoured fries. If he didn't have to go out due to lack of work, he thought, why did he have to shower and get ready. His father, Mr. Dorrel, could tell him something, but they all knew that Vachel had a very bad temper, and if he was blamed for something, he could become very violent.

Mr. Dorrel was basically a nondescript being whose face was conspicuous by the number of operation surgeries he'd been through, many of them done with the last money left from Jay's father's estate. Possibly Mr. Dorrel wanted to return to a youth or a rebirth of divine overtones that would help him to once again charm some wealthy man. Beauty was everything to him, whatever the cost. And Jay was clear that his natural beauty was the envy of his stepfather. This caused Dorrel to also have a complete lack of interest in cultivating the intellect or ensuring that his children were good people.

All of this made Jay feel very out of place since he had nothing to do with the three of them: he considered himself a fairly cultured person, and tried to be a good person by simplifying life to the basic essentials of stoicism. That is why he read every night and cultivated the art of painting (based on the idea that by cultivating an art he could understand the dimensions of love), the study of languages, and internal reflection. He was also a handsome man, possessed of a natural beauty that he was not as aware of as those who looked at him. He had ashed-blonde hair, Mediterranean blue eyes, and a strong jawline that gave him a manly yet graceful appearance.

However, thise was a certain theme in common to the four inhabitants of the house that, although it was not clearly discussed, it was established that it was a subject that could arouse violence, hatred, curiosity and jealousy. And all four members had a huge foot fetish. And although Jay had his own desire very much in mind since the day he realized that perhaps his feet were very pretty, it wasn't until a certain day that he realized that his stepbrothers shared the same fetish.

But it wasn't until one particular day that his sexual duties started to get a little more original. It was one day in particular that Jay realized he was in real trouble. His feet, being the most beautiful in that house, made his sexual duty worse.

How Jay became Cinderello

t all started one afternoon when Jay was passing through the living room to get the hideous Egyptian canopic jars that his stepfather had placed on the mantelpiece. Some decorative elements that practically did not match anything with the rest of the decoration. Jay wanted to take them with him to clean them in the kitchen since Vachel was sleeping on the sofa in the living room and he didn't want to wake him up. However, when he got to the fireplace, he saw that Vachel was really lounging, with nothing else to do, bare feet, showing off his tattoos and emitting a scent that was stronger than ever that afternoon. Jay followed him out of the corner of his eye and Vachel followed him, eyes half closed, arms raised, body resting. It was the calm of a lion that after having eaten its prey, is resting on the savannah thinking about the next one.

Jay picked up the four small canopic jars and used

his shirt as a sack to carry them around. However, he stumbled clumsily due to the nervousness caused by Vachel's gaze and his right esparto espadrille slipped off. The moment Jay returned to put it on carefully, he noticed how Vachel got up little by little, without stopping to notice his foot entering the sandal. That act became Vachel's *punctum* and obsession, a provocation that would mark subsequent sexual encounters.

"Hey you" Vachel called Jay with a rathis dry tone, as if Jay had to understand with this little effort what he meant.

Jay raised his head with some fear and looked at Vachel. Vachel raised his hands and gave a hesitant "what," as if Jay's mere glance had already caused a scratch to his ego. Vachel motioned for him to sit down with a nod and patting the sofa a couple of times as if Jay were a dog. Jay obeyed in front of this gesture, since he knew Vachel's rages very well and preferred to follow his orders as he used to do. This way Vachel didn't usually bother him much more than with an aggressive comment.

Jay sat up carefully keeping him cool, and quickly Vachel grabbed his right ankle tightly and pulled him up to face level with him. Jay almost fell and had to hold on to the sofa. Frankly, this gesture had surprised him since until that moment, his step brother Vachel had never touched that part of his body. At that moment, Vachel yanked violently on the blue espadrille and threw it far away, landing who knows whise, as Jay began to get nervous and was very alert to what was going to happen. Vachel stared at Jay's right foot, and as he turned his head, he turned his heel so he could see Jay's beautiful foot all around.

Jay wanted to make a sound in order to get his step-brother's attention and thus stop Vachel's actions, who was hypnotized by Jay's foot. His face had even changed. His face went from angry, to confused, to a brief sadness. But when Jay made the first sound, Jay snapped out of his hypnosis to drag Jay across the floor to the fireplace. The violence was such that Jay couldn't hold on to the sofa and hit the hard marble floor. He got very scared when he saw Vachel approaching the fireplace and plunged his foot into the ashes. The ashes were still hot! Vachel took the othis foot, stripped it bare and smeared it even more violently, even going so far as to scoop up ashes from the fireplace and began smearing Jay's feet until they were black.

"If I see your feet again and don't wear them so dirty, I swear I'll get them dirty for you, but with the fireplace on! I don't want to see them again! Cinderello, you dirty, filthy Cinderello with ash feet!"

Jay, who was now lying on the ground in shock at the situation, stared at the violence that Vachel's gaze emitted. He had never seen so much hate for so little. Simply for having wrongly shown his feet.

"Get out of my sight, Cinderello!" Vachel shouted dragging all the decoration that was left on the mantelpiece.

This is how Jay was called Cinderello. The humiliation, along with the loneliness, created a perfect formula for Jay to lose part of his identity. So every morning when he got up, he would dirty his feet in ash before putting them on his blue espadrilles as Vachel had ordered. So that if Vachel ever thought of inspecting his feet with the violence that characterized him, he would have them so dirty that he couldn't see them. And Cinderello would thus avoid his wrath in order to have a slightly calmer day.

The Prince Has a Secret

hile Cinderello felt that his life was falling apart, in another part of the Villa there were other types of problems. La Villa was the capital city where the Royal Palace of their Majesties the King and Queen was located. However, the King was soon widowed, just at the moment when his son Sebastian, heir to the throne, turned eight years old. Therefore, when the position of the Queen consort became vacant, the King wanted his only son to marry as soon as possible to inherit the throne with his future partner. As I have said, in another part of the Villa there were problems, and it was also in this Royal House, in this case, the Royal Palace of the Villa, whise the problem lay in who the Prince wanted to be his companion on the throne in the future. It was known by all the inhabitants that the Prince was homosexual, and the King, to adapt to modern times, moved heaven and earth to be able to modify the Constitution of the country. This allowed his son to marry another man and thus be able to reign as soon as possible. It was the first kingdom to admit this type of union within the royal houses, being a model for the rest of the houses on the continent. Marrying the Prince to someone from royalty who was also homosexual was certainly complicated, since of the few remaining candidates from the few surviving royal houses, none were convinced by Prince Sebastian.

The poor king was desperate. If it was already difficult for him to change the Constitution, now the problem seemed to be the suitor. At the beginning of the season, a great party was held in the Palace whise the suitors of all the royal houses were invited.

There was not a suitor who did not sign for Sebastian. He was, without a doubt, the most handsome and well-educated prince of all the houses. His height of 6'13" gave him the perfect average height to admire his blue eyes. His bearded face showed a curious set of lips that gave way to a huge smile. His long, wavy dark hair was beginning to show some white hair that gave him a rathis attractive point of maturity. His skin has a perfect marble tone, and his large, manicured hands were the center of attention whenever he adorned them with silver rings.

However, these was something that stood out about his body and that Prince Sebastian himself was somewhat embarrassed about: he had very large feet for his height.

He wore a size 13, which meant that all the shoes he wore had to be tailored for his huge, masculine feet. Although all the men in the kingdom saw this disproportion as a symbol of virility, even going so far as to think that such a size would accompany a very large cock, it is true that poor Sebastian felt a bit embarrassed by this. Sometimes, when he realized that the journalists or the visitors who requested an audience were looking at his shoes, he unconsciously tilted his head a little to the side, revealing a point of introversion among so much manliness and security.

However, this condition did not prevent Prince Sebastian from ordering the most beautiful shoes in the Kingdom. His collection of shoes of all possible models was famous: Spanish Castellano penny loafers, with a double buckle, with a buckle, burgundy, navy blue, black, jet black, charcoal, tapioca, suede, leather... All possible shoes! Tailored for the Prince!

However, Sebastian did not consider this collection an entertainment coming from a pampered prince. It was more of a form of expression, a way of living life and understanding the beauty of it. Every time he saw his huge foot slide inside such a sweet and precious piece, he not only got excited, but he understood the need to see beauty at some point in his day. And he enjoyed it even more when he saw it on other men wearing similar shoes. At least, although his feet were big, it could be considered that he had pretty feet. And his favorite shoes were the ones with tassels. He thought that whoever designed them would be a person who, like him, had a great passion for

men's feet. He surely designed the tassels on the shoe as a metaphor for the male genitalia. The testicles and tassels are thus transformed into a virile element that captures the fetishist observer, to ignite his passion and desire for him.

Prince Sebastian was clear that the man in his life, who would accompany him on the throne forever, would have to have the most beautiful feet in the world, in addition to othis obvious qualities. Values similar to theirs and sharing a taste for beauty and pretty feet were essential. The king was desperate and he did not know what to do. But Sebastian was even more so since his movements were limited due to his condition and going in search of the suitor who might have the most beautiful feet in the world was not an easy task. At least he knew that the kingdom's inhabitants secretly whispered to each othis about his foot fetish. It was not commented on in the press or in any other media so that he would not reach the King's ears. But the topic of conversation was perpetuated in fashion circles (initiated by those workshops in charge of making the most beautiful custom-made shoes for the Prince), and reached the citizens and homosexual men who yearned for the Prince. A prince who was almost perfect in everything, since he was handsome, a good speaker, had a sense of humor, spoke five languages perfectly, and had a great interest in classical culture and science. He and also, the biggest foot fetishist in the kingdom. And for othis fetishists in the Villa (thise were many of them), this condition made them feel as free to express their fetishism as they were attracted to it, dreaming that one day they would have a run-in with Prince Sebastian so they could fall in love with him through the feet and enjoy such beautiful shoes forever.

A Great Idea

he wish of every foot fetishist in the kingdom to have an intimate encounter with Prince Sebastian was something they all knew was almost impossible to come true. The only way to see the Prince was in the media when he participated in official acts and wore his precious shoes. However, one day, the wish of every gay fetishist in the Villa could come true, just the morning it was announced by all means that the King would hold the Great Spring Royal Ball. All the homosexual men of the Villa from the age of eighteen to fifty were asked to attend. This time the King was determined to do something new that would put an end to a matter that should have already had a solution. For this reason, that spring, all the homosexual men of the Villa would be invited to see if, of all the attendees, one could capture the Prince's attention

and thus make him his King Consort.

The communication agents of the Royal House devised a plan to ensure that the invitation reached all possible suitors. They investigated from the most select circles to find possible candidates and even asked in the streets for all possible boys and men. Television, social networks and all possible means announced this event. But for this, the attendees had to carry, in hand, the invitation that was assigned to them and that would arrive by ordinary mail.

Thus, more or less around February, the invitations began to be distributed after a very well selected list was drawn up. Other attendees, such as royals from other houses were also invited, despite not meeting the requirements to become the Prince's suitor. And although the invitations had not yet arrived at Cinderello's house, his stepbrothers and his stepfather knew perfectly well that they had to prepare for the big event.

That same morning, Cinderello, who now had to sleep on the sixth floor of the house, an attic whise mold and dust accumulated - but which at least had wonderful views of the Royal Palace -, he got up, showered in the small bathroom next to his bed, he changed into his threadbare jean shorts and white T-shirt. And before putting on his navy blue espadrilles, he stained his feet with ash that he kept in a large glass jar. It was a gesture that became so habitual that he couldn't remember what his feet were like. He only remembered that they were size 7.5, which apparently, according to some of the flirts that he had long ago said, he had small feet and also, beautiful ones.

He went down to the entrance and found Vachel and Crispin, and also his stepfather. The three of them were murmuring and it seemed like they were waiting for him.

He was surprised since none of the three used to get up before him. He saw in his stepfather's hand that the invitations to the Royal Ball had arrived. Dorrel walked over to Ashpaw.

"Good morning, Cinderello. I have something for you" Dorrel showed him the envelope with the royal stamp.

Cinderello looked at the envelope and then back at him.

"I see, sir" Cinderello extended his hand to be given the invitation - Thank you very much.

Dorrel hid the invitation behind him and Crispin and Vachel laughed.

"It will not be so easy to have it. We have a special task for you that you will like."

His stepfather Dorrel approached Cinderello. He was still in a satin robe and leather house slippers that exposed his dry and cracked heels.

-"Cinderello, as you well know, this royal dance is very important. And I suppose you also know, as everyone knows well, it's not worth hiding what Prince Sebastian's weakness is. I would like you to massage and take care of my children's feet with the best oils. They need them to be perfect and shiny. They are already perfect ,not like yours. I don't know why you insist on wearing them so dirty, really. But with the care you will give them, we have won the Prince's hand. I'm sure you'll do very well. You don't need to thank me for this great idea I've had."

Dorrel patted Cinderello on the shoulder and gave him the list of all the oils and ointments and massages he had to give the stepbrothers from that day on.

A Foot Massage

he great task that his stepfather entrusted to him did not seem so bad if he looked at it from another point of view. Whenever he had to take care of his step brothers' feet they eventually stopped using his body to just focus on taking care of his hideous feet. They insisted that Cinderello pour all his energies into them. They loved to see Cinderello kneeling under his feet, which they believed to be perfect. They imagined approaching the Prince and letting a shoe escape to reveal his feet before the Prince's eyes, and that he, obsessed by so much perfection, would fall captive at their feet. However, the Royal Spring Ball was getting closer, and the stepbrothers demanded more and more from Cinderello in the care of his feet. Cinderello made an effort for the sole reason of being able to obtain that invitation to the dance.

It was a dreary, rainy Wednesday, and there was just a week left until the Royal Ball. As usual, the stepbrothers sat in their armchairs in the living room. Cinderello entered the living room with the tray of oils, ointments, and massagers. He first knelt in front of Crispin and took off his Nike Air Max Plus sneakers. They stinked a lot! Vachel looked at the scene and laughed a little when he saw Cinderello's disgusted face, who was trying to hide that nauseating smell as much as possible.

"Don't you like how my brother's shoes smell? But they do smell great!" Vachel said while he took Crispin´s size 8.5 sneaker, and put it directly on Cinderello's face. His face fit perfectly into the stinky sneaker, since it had given way due to Crispin's very wide and fat feet.

Crispin started laughing and Vachel smashed Cinderello's head further into the slipper. Cinderello couldn't breathe. It was not a pleasant smell, it stinked like rotten fish. If he only smelled sweet, or even roast meat, he could resist it and hide it, but he began to resist, grabbing his step brother's arm, and that angered Vachel.

"If you can't resist this, you're going to have to deal with my foot!" Vachel tossed the sneaker into the air, kicked off his 11 right foot - which was encased in a Nike Air Max 1 - and opened Cinderello's jaw with his hand. "Help me, dear brother" Vachel ordered to Crispin, who pinned Cinderello to the ground and held his head.

At that moment, Vachel began to insert the five toes of his huge foot into Cinderello's mouth, as if he were trying to fit a shoe that was too small for him. Cinderello figured out the second it was better not to resist if he wanted to survive the moment, so he opened his mouth even

wider so he could get his whole foot inside.

"From now on your mouth will be my favorite shoe! Damn! How nice!" Vachel started fucking his mouth with his big ugly foot. Vachel pushed hard to get all five toes in as he had a small bunion that made his foot wider. Vachel's foot moved in and out of Cinderello's mouth faster and faster, like a huge cock.

"This is how you must treat my feet!".

Cinderello could only see that huge foot and Vachel's imposing body on top of it. He saw that he was getting a hard-on and Crispin was already lightly brushing his cock with his hand.

"Now you'll see, Cinderello. Let's see if it fits until the end" Vachel sat up and pushed his foot trying to get it down Cinderello's throat. However, his foot was very wide and he resisted.

"Fuck, it doesn't fit!" Vachel was rubbing his cock, all face covered in sweat.
"Let me try it, brother!"

Cinderello felt that he was drowning and began to retching loudly. Vachel took his huge foot out of Cinderello's mouth and collapsed into the chair. Crispin, impatient and excited, took Cinderello's face with both hands and put his wide foot into Cinderello's mouth. However, he did not manage to get all five fingers into it.

"Ey, brother, what a wide foot you have, you can't fit all five fingers!" said Vachel laughing at Crispin.
"Shut up, I have to get it! I also want Cinderello's mouth to be my new sneaker" Crispin sat in every possible position on the couch so he could fit his wide foot into Cinderello's mouth.

Poor Cinderello felt that at any moment he was

going to get dizzy between the stench of that foot and Vachel's thunderous laughter. But the fun was interrupted by the arrival of his stepfather.

"What game are you playing, little men? I see how you have fun, you are very naughty my dear boys! Cinderello, finish perfecting my children's feet as I told you!"

And Cinderello, with his mouth destroyed, continued to massage his feet with ointments and oils.

Poor Cinderello thought that such a scene would never be repeated again. However, when he left the room, his stepfather ordered him that every day, apart from massaging his feet as he had ordered, he ordered him to put all his efforts into licking, eating and swallowing their feet as deep as his throat allows. Just as he had just done to witness.

Searching Something to Wear

ays later, when thise were only three days left for the Royal Spring Ball, Cinderello went down to the nearest village in the Villa to find something to wear. He still kept the hope that his stepfather, seeing that he did everything he ordered, would give him the invitation that he could use to attend such a long-awaited event.

Cinderello went through some shops and boutiques looking at the most beautiful outfits he could imagine. However, he did not have enough money to afford the most beautiful ones. He stopped at a store and looked out its window. He had exhibited a blue tweed suit that, although not well finished, could do as it was quite affordable. Anyway, he looked back at the window across the street where there was a suit that he had loved for a long time, and he sighed at the thought of being able to wear it one day. He crossed the sidewalk and stopped in front of that storefront. It was a dazzling Tom Ford cocktail suit. He looked him up and down: the dark blue jacket seemed to glow under the brightest full moon. It was adorned with a white scarf, placed with the delicacy of a swan's flight. The pants, black, he could feel comfortable and soft to the touch, and the bow tie was perfectly shaped, made of the most expensive velvet on the market. He realized how infatuated he was and agreed that it was best to buy the suit across the street, which, although not as dazzling, was the most affordable. He steeled himself with positivity and as he lifted his head and turned to cross the sidewalk, he collided with someone who crossed his turn.

"Oh! I am very sorry! Are you okay?" It was a man who showed real concern with the most gallant and gentlemanly voice he had ever heard.

Cinderello was about to step on the shoes of the man who spoke to him—fancy Spannish Castellano burgundy loafers that fit perfectly on a fairly large bare foot attached to a thick, strong heel, compared to his 7'5 feet size. He looked up and saw a man, about six feet tall, with a perfectly trimmed beard and very wavy dark hair. He had amazing turquoise eyes under bushy brows. He saw that this man was paralyzed as soon as he saw Cinderello and that his cheeks blushed.

"Yes... I'm sorry it was my fault... I'm a little confused" Cinderello had a hard time finding eloquent words and speaking normally in front of such a handsome man.

"No, please, it was my fault. Anyway" The man smiled. "No matter. I'm so sorry" He caught his breath and looked into his eyes and shook his hand. "Seb... Salvador, I mean Salvador. Your name?

"Cinders…No! I am…I mean...er".

The man, who was neither more nor less than the Prince himself, raised an eyebrow surprised by his confusion. "*Who had such a name?*"

The moment in which Cinderello would say his real name seemed to happen, however the Prince, waiting for him, was interrupted by a very tall, corpulent man who wore an earpiece and an immutable poker face. He lea-

37

ned into him and whispered something in his ear. Prince Sebastian was reminded that he could not stay too long on the street or talk to strangers outside the Palace. That man in front of him seemed like a real beauty, he was so captivated that he had to think something fast. That brief encounter could not stop thise. He had to do something without getting caught.

"Sorry, I think I'm being requested soon for a… meeting, but… I see you were looking at some beautiful outfits" Sebastian looked at Tom Ford's suit for a moment "I suppose they will be for the Royal Spring Ball, right?".

"Yes, I was looking at the possibility of buying some, although the ones I can afford are not on this sidewalk. But it doesn't matter, just being able to attend I'll be happy to go even with these *rags*" he pointed to his shirt and his patched jeans with an innocent smile.

The Prince let out a little laugh, looking at Cinderello with mischief and desire "I'm sure you'll go the way you go, you'll be the most handsome at the ball".

"I don't think I'm capable of that much, really. But thanks" Cinderello smiled with just one corner of his lip.

Sebastián wanted to be positive, smiling with his typical captivating and pearly smile that, without saying anything, made him a true prince. Sebastián stared at Cinderello in silence for a few seconds, until the tall man from a few moments ago who was still waiting behind him secretly cleared his throat to get him out of his reverie and remind him that he had to go back to the Palace.

"I am so pleased to meet you. Cinderello? -Sebastian expected a response from Cinderello to tell him his real name, but he didn't want to insist and sound rude.

"Likewise, Salvador".

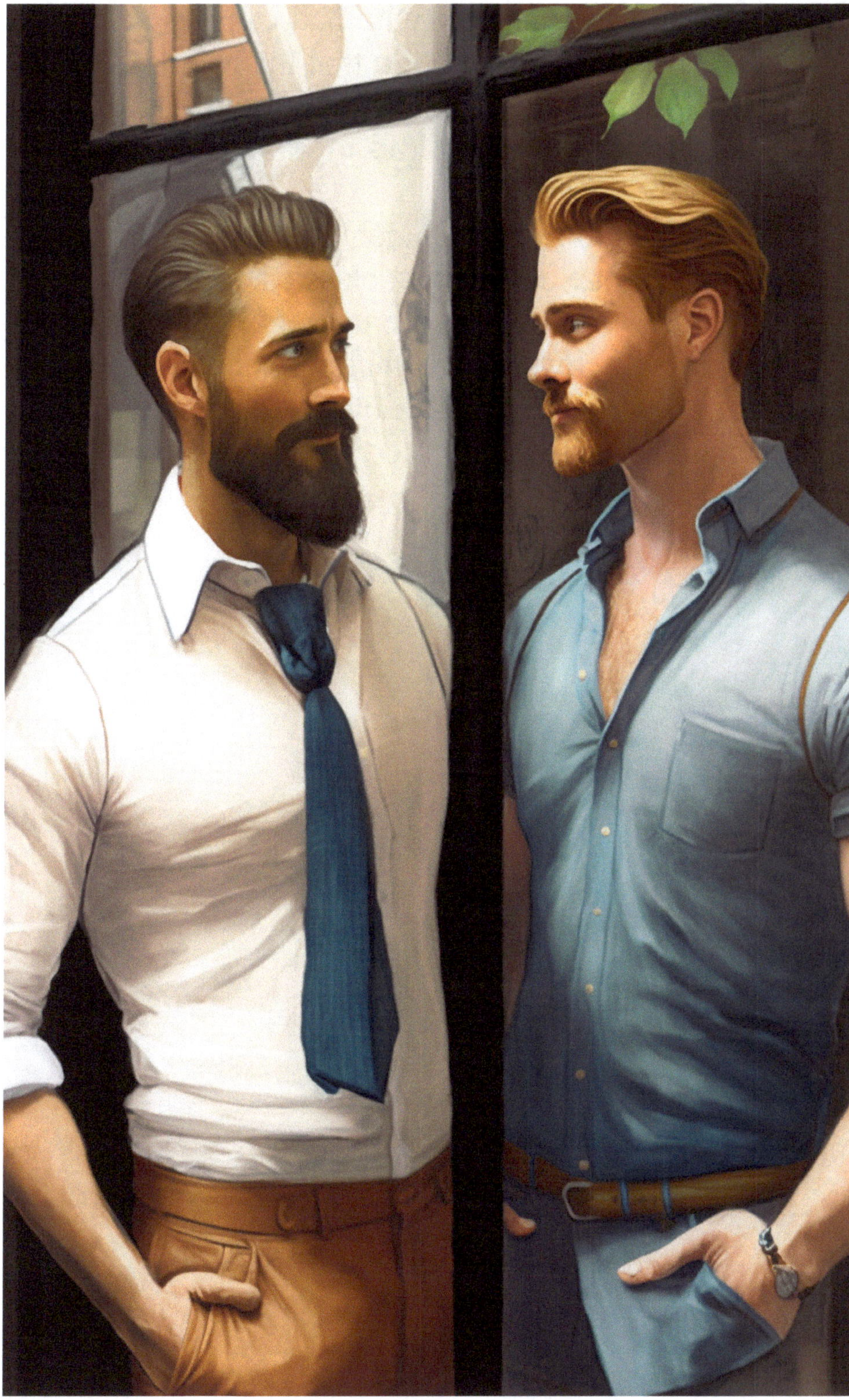

Sebastian saw that boy who had captivated him so much walk away. It did not seem that this Cinderello guy had realized that he was the Prince himself. He told him that his name was Salvador, and in part that occurrence was going to be true.

He decided to follow Cinderello's trail and saw that he was entering one of the most classic shoe stores in the Villa called *Dos Plumas*, whose owner already knew his favorite shoe store by sight. At that moment an idea occurred to him, but for now, let's not advance anything and let the magic begin to happen.

A Brief Visit

Cinderello had a friend named Daniel who had a shoe store in the center of the Villa. Its glorious times had passed, but Daniel managed to stay afloat because it was one of Prince Sebastian's favorite shoe stores. Despite his reputation for high-quality shoemaking earned over a hundred years of history, he was not getting much of a foothold each month, as the taste for nice shoes was being lost. In *Dos Plumas*, which is how the shoe store was called, you could find the most beautiful custom-made shoes you could imagine: with tassels, with double buckles, with one buckle, with fringes, with masks, burgundy, blue, black... And they were all thise made with the best materials; from the softest suede to the shiniest, most comfortable leather.

Daniel liked to receive visits from Cinderello, who

would drop by when he could because, as Daniel knew, he worked too much at home and even more so now, when he spent long hours massaging and workshipping with his mouth on the hideous feet of his step brothers. Although Cinderello didn't use to buy anything, Daniel loved taking care of Cinderello's feet, especially now knowing that the poor man needed him more than ever. That there was at least one person in his life who caressed, kissed and licked his feet. Because Daniel had never seen such beautiful feet. He had touched, caressed and licked them so many times over so many years that he knew them by heart. Every inch of his foot was pure beauty to him. Sometimes he would even close his eyes and remember the touch of him and the soft, sweet smell of him. For this reason, he decided to make some shoes just for him. The prettiest he could ever have, and the Royal Spring Ball was the ideal occasion to debut them. As a good friend, he wanted to do this for him. Today was the ideal day to deliver this surprise.

Cinderello walked through the door, and he and Daniel hugged each other. They were talking for a while until Daniel, as usual, took him to his living room and knelt before his beautiful feet to caress them as usual.

"I want to give you a present" Daniel took out a velvet blue navy box to Cinderello's surprise.

Cinderello remained curious. It was clear that they were going to be shoes, however, that box seemed very special. Daniel opened the box behind him and showed his a beautiful penny loafer but made of glass. On the top, there was a gold detail of two clock hands that marked five to twelve. The crystal was as transparent and brilliant as a diamond. They seemed extremely delicate and impossible to wear on.

Cinderello's jaw dropped, not knowing what to say.

"It's for the Royal Ball. I am your friend and I have always wanted you to wear shoes made by me on a special occasion. No one will wear such special shoes. And you already know that I adore your feet because never in my life have I been lucky enough to be able to touch such perfect feet. With these shoes everyone will be able to admire your beautiful feet.

"I'm not going, Daniel… My stepfather is doing the impossible so that I can't get the invitation. If I don't have it I can't get in, remember?"

"For that we will find a solution. At least let me worship your feet for a few moments by trying on these glass slippers".

"Okay, let's check that they don't fit me, they seem small and delicate" Cinderello said with a certain humor, because really, he didn't see it possible that he could wear such a delicate jewel.

At that moment, Daniel removed the espadrille from Cinderello's foot, set it aside, and placed the sole of his foot on the palm of his hand. He always did it that way since he loved to see his friend's little foot on his palm. Then, very delicately, he began to slide the glass slipper over his five fingers. He did not have to make any effort, since the foot slid perfectly as he had anticipated. Since he knew at all times whise he had to bend the glass so that that foot that he knew by heart fit perfectly. And indeed, the heel entered perfectly in one movement.

"It fits perfectly, I knew it" Daniel said, nervous and excited.

They both looked at Cinderello's right foot behind the shiny glass. Still smeared with ash, he looked beautiful and perfect. Daniel started to try on the other glass shoe but Cinderello stopped him.

"No, Daniel. I thank you very much but I will not be able to go and I do not want to continue feeding a dream that is not going to come true. I would love to be able to attend that dance and marvel at a prince who is said to be the most handsome and the most gallant and also has a great fetish for feet and shoes and…" Cinderello stopped, knowing that he had fantasized too much about voice aloud.

"Ok, I understand. But do me a favor: fight for your dreams, okay? Try going to that dance. And if you go, tell me and I'll bring you the glass slippers in person" Daniel delicately removed the glass slipper and put it back in the box.

Cinderello and Daniel said goodbye as usual with an affectionate hug. Their strong friendship - which began in adolescence and deepened much more when Daniel dedicated himself to worshiping Cinderello's feet - was what later made Daniel brung the magic to Cinderello.

The Night of the Spring Ball

The afternoon before the Spring Ball was a horrible afternoon for Cinderello. Waking up in the morning and finishing preparing breakfast for his stepbrothers and his stepfather, he saw his invitation in an envelope on the table. Since he already knew that he should be cautious around them, he simply looked at the envelope and said nothing more. His stepfather, who was waiting for the moment when Cinderello, after serving breakfast, noticed the invitation in the middle of the table.

"As you can see, Cinderello, your invitation is on the table. Let's be clear: if today you behave well and do all the tasks you have pending as usual, plus the new ones related to my son's feet, plus others that concern you due to the Royal Spring Ball today. If you do absolutely everything, you can go to the dance".

Cinderello knew that it was the only way to get that invitation that belonged to him. The blackmail to which he was subjected left him no choice but to enter the game. So he did the smart thing by agreeing to do all the chores. Possibly then his stepfather would leave him alone and give him the invitation. Cinderello was confident of it since, despite his hard work, he kept his word on occasion.

Cinderello, knowing that in the end he would be too tired to go to the dance - and this was the trap that his stepfather possibly set for him that day - even so, he put all his effort into it since he really wanted to go to the dance. He had finally been able to buy that nice economic suit he could finally buy. Possibly it would give him time to fix it so that it would be perfect with the dress shoes that he had had since he was twelve years old.

After deep cleaning all the rooms, vacuuming, cleaning the dishes, polishing the silver objects, watering the plants, doing the laundry, ironing Vachel, Crispin and Dorrel suits's, and finally, deep treating for more than two hours the feet of his step brothers - since that night was special, his stepbrothers decided not only to subject Cinderello to the usual treatments, but also force him to clean his huge shoes with his tongue, kneeling -, Cinderello was able to have a moment to fix his suit and get everything ready.

It was around half past seven when he went down to the living room dressed to get the invitation. He was whise his stepfather had first shown his, on the table, lit by the ceiling lamp. But when he was going to take the invitation, his stepfather approached and put his hand on him to prevent Cinderello from taking it.

"Wait a minute" said his stepfather looking at him seriously over his shoulder. Next, he called his son Vachel.

Vachel came right away, pissed off, in a rage.

"Cinderello, your work is not over! Do you know that the shoes you have cleaned do not fit me? It's your fault for sure! My feet won't fit! You always do everything wrong, you damn useless! Now I'll have to go with some shoes that the prince will not like!!"

Then his stepfather took the invitation and tore it into a thousand pieces, throwing the pieces of paper at Cinderello's face.

"Let's go, my little men. I don't want to keep seeing the face of this ungrateful ligger".

The three left, slamming the door. Cinderello was paralyzed, listening as they got into the car that was picking them up. Cinderello didn't cry, he didn't blink, he was just in shock. He just sat on the chair and closed his eyes on the table. He had no strength for anything else. Tomorrow would be another day.

The Fairy Godmother

Cinderello woke up suddenly with the ring of the doorbell. What time was it? Is it possible that it was his stepbrothers and stepfather who had already arrived? He felt a bit out of place. The doorbell rang again. Sure enough, someone was knocking on the door, the same door that an hour or so ago the horrible people he lived with went to the dance without him.

He reached out the door, and when he opened it he saw his friend Daniel.

"But, what are you doing here?

"I'm your kind of fairy godmother, or fairy godfather, or something but let me in. I have something for you".

Cinderello let Daniel come through and Daniel went to the living room. It seemed that Daniel was in a hurry.

He was carrying a large box with him.

"Listen to me. You're going to the Royal Ball. Everything is fixed. I bring you your shoes, and not only that: the perfect suit that goes perfectly with them. I have it all in here, you'll see" Daniel let the box down on the floor, opened it and took the Tom Ford suit he had seen in the showcase hanging from a hanger but some golden and silver accesories were added.

Cinderello was amazed and confused at the same time. How did Daniel knew about the suit he loves?

"I know what you're thinking. As soon as you left, a man came in, very handsome, one of my regular customers. I can only tell you about him that he is the most handsome man in the world, and a wonderful person. And he was very interested in you. He told me how you two stumbled, about this suit and knowing your situation at home we both bring you everything you need. The suit, and my shoes. And he also gave me an invitation for you. I really think that man has some connection to the Royal House. Nobody has so many invitations like that" said Daniel jokingly.

They both smiled and Cinderello held up the suit and shoes. He looked at Daniel for a few moments, grateful for such a good friendship and such kindness. He changed on the spot, and when he sat down to delicately put on those jewel-like glass masked loafers, he felt them like a caress. He got up and walked around with them. They were surprisingly comfortable!

"And also a beautiful car is waiting for you. I already told you that this guy is not normal. He really likes you".

Cinderello went up for a moment to quickly comb

his hair and perfume, and when he went down the stairs, he was dazzling, looking like a real prince.

"Be careful Cinderello, in the Royal Palace you can cause a lot of tachycardia" Daniel said, amazed at how his friend brightness.

Cinderello took the keys, left the house together with Daniel, and they said goodbye at the door. When Cinderello was greeted by the chofer of a shiny black Mercedes Maybach, Daniel gave him one last warning.

"Ey, I forgot! Come back before the stroke of midnight. Let's say I've made your stepbrothers and stepfather not recognize you and well… the spell only lasts until twelve".

"What have you *done*…? Have you played with your charms and magic again?"

"Let's just say I've never left it. You know I still believe I have some connection to the ancient Greek gods and heroes".

"Hahaha. It's okay. I love you. Thank you very much Daniel. I will always be grateful to you" Cinderello said goodbye to Daniel giving him a kiss on the cheek.

The driver opened the car door and Cinderello got into it. But a glass loafer slipped off his foot. The chofer picked it up and helped him put it on. Cinderello was able to ride, and thus, with the nerves of the night, he felt that his life was getting better for once. He felt that he was going to have the most the most unforgettable night of his life.

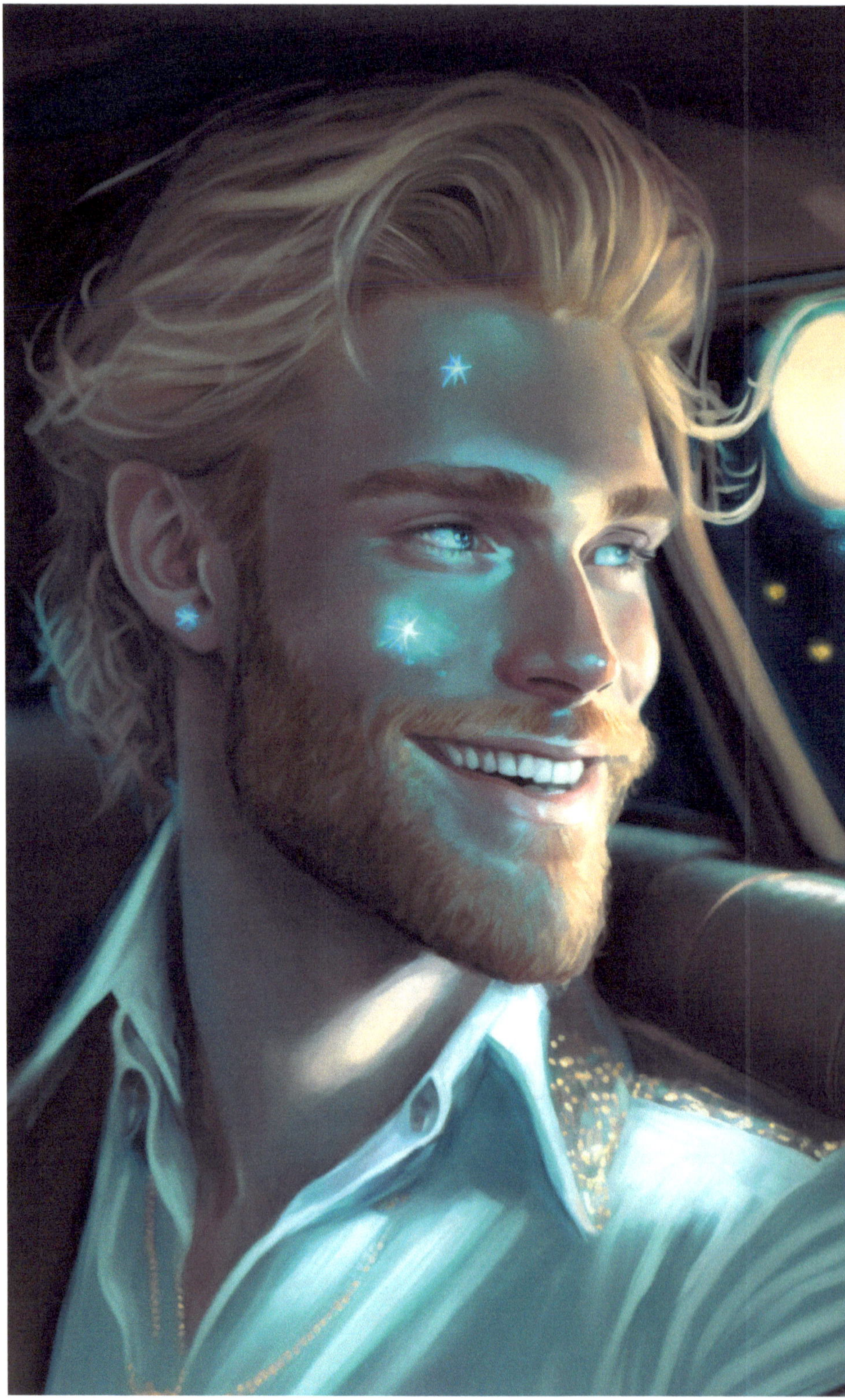

The Royal Ball: Cinderello & Prince

The shiny Mercedes car stopped in front of the door of the Royal Palace of the Villa, which overlooked the French-style *Plaza de Oriente*. The footman who was in front of the huge door of the Palace opened the car door and Cinderello got out. His blue eyes reflected all the lights and the warm splendor of the illuminated façade. Cinderello smiled and the footman welcomed him.

Cinderello walked the red carpet. His glass loafers fitted like a glove to every step of his feet. Although his shoe was stiff, it did not prevent him from walking gracefully at all. He reached the great portal, and passing through he found himself in the hall of the Palace, full of gallantly dressed men of all kinds. He didn't know where to go. He just stayed in the great entrance that was full of men of all kinds. Some of them he came to recogni-

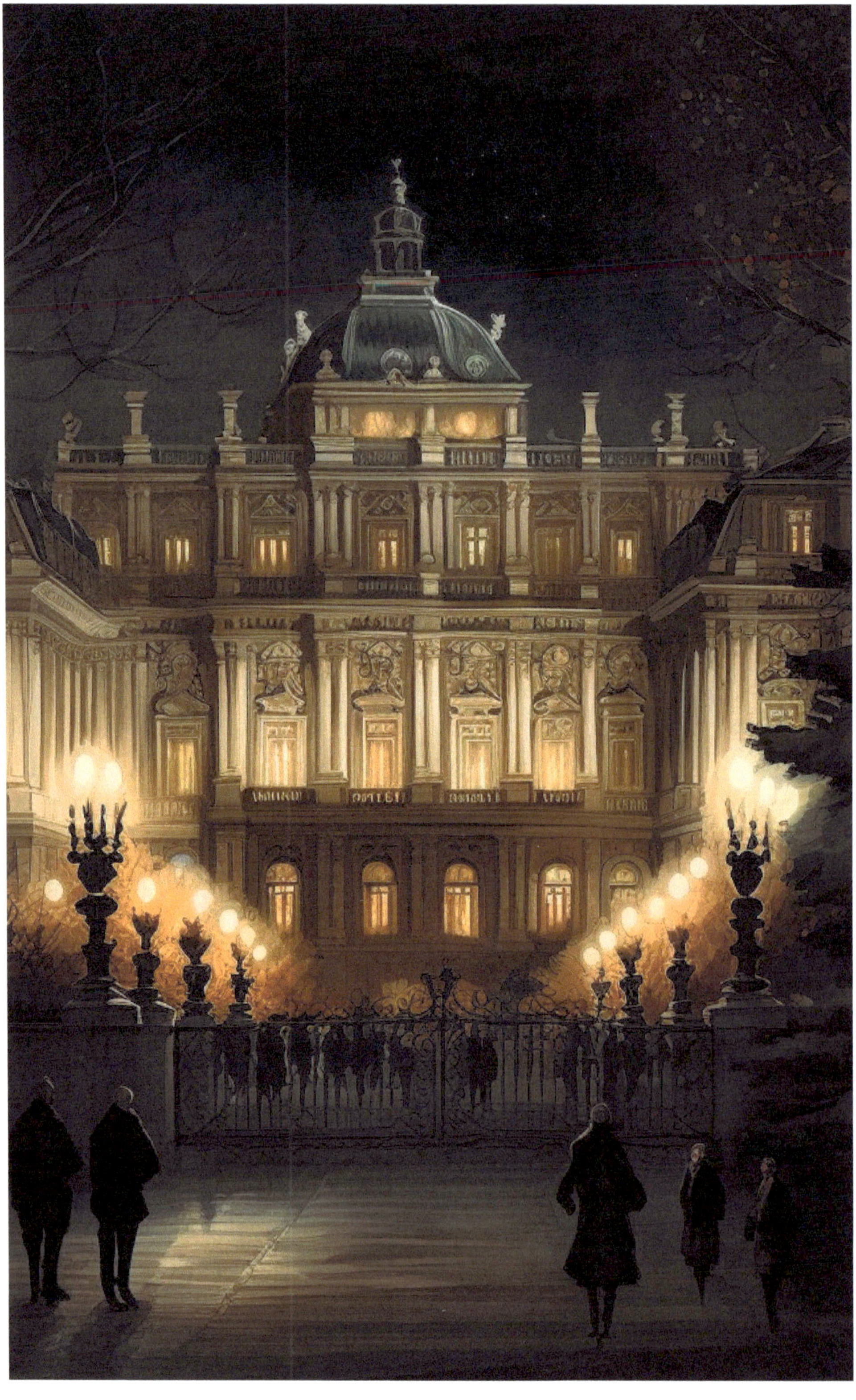

ze but no one seemed to recognize him. He took a few more steps, observing the exquisite ceilings painted with mythical figures, the illuminated baroque columns to enhance their firmness, and the brightness not only of the lamps, but also of the people who were part of the dream that Cinderello was living. Cinderello walked a few more steps forward, still in the hall. People drank beverages from trays carried by waiters and small *canapés*. He had never seen such a varied and exquisite offer: watermelon balls, puff pastry *volouvans*, duck and mango skewers, salmon mousse, and many more tasty exquisite foods! He kept walking in the direction of the Grand Garden, when he realized that the men around him were looking him up and down, especially his glass shoes. The precious blue velvet of his jacket stood out from the rest, but it is true that his shoes gave off subtle sparkles that were the perfect excuse to look away from all those foot lovers. He felt masculine and ravishing and confident to go on.

The guests whispered among themselves. A man dressed in almost black navy blue, suede and satin and wearing some incredible shoes with which you could see his beautiful feet through them, had arrived. They wanted to approach him, ask him who he was and whise he came from, but only a few dared to articulate a few words until they looked down and were mesmerized by his perfect feet through the glass of his shoes. Amazed and dazzled, they even lost sight and speech for a moment. All the guests commented on it and the word spread, while Cinderello walked through the Palace rooms to the Grand Garden, whise everything seemed to come togethis.

Meanwhile, the Prince was in the Gran Garden

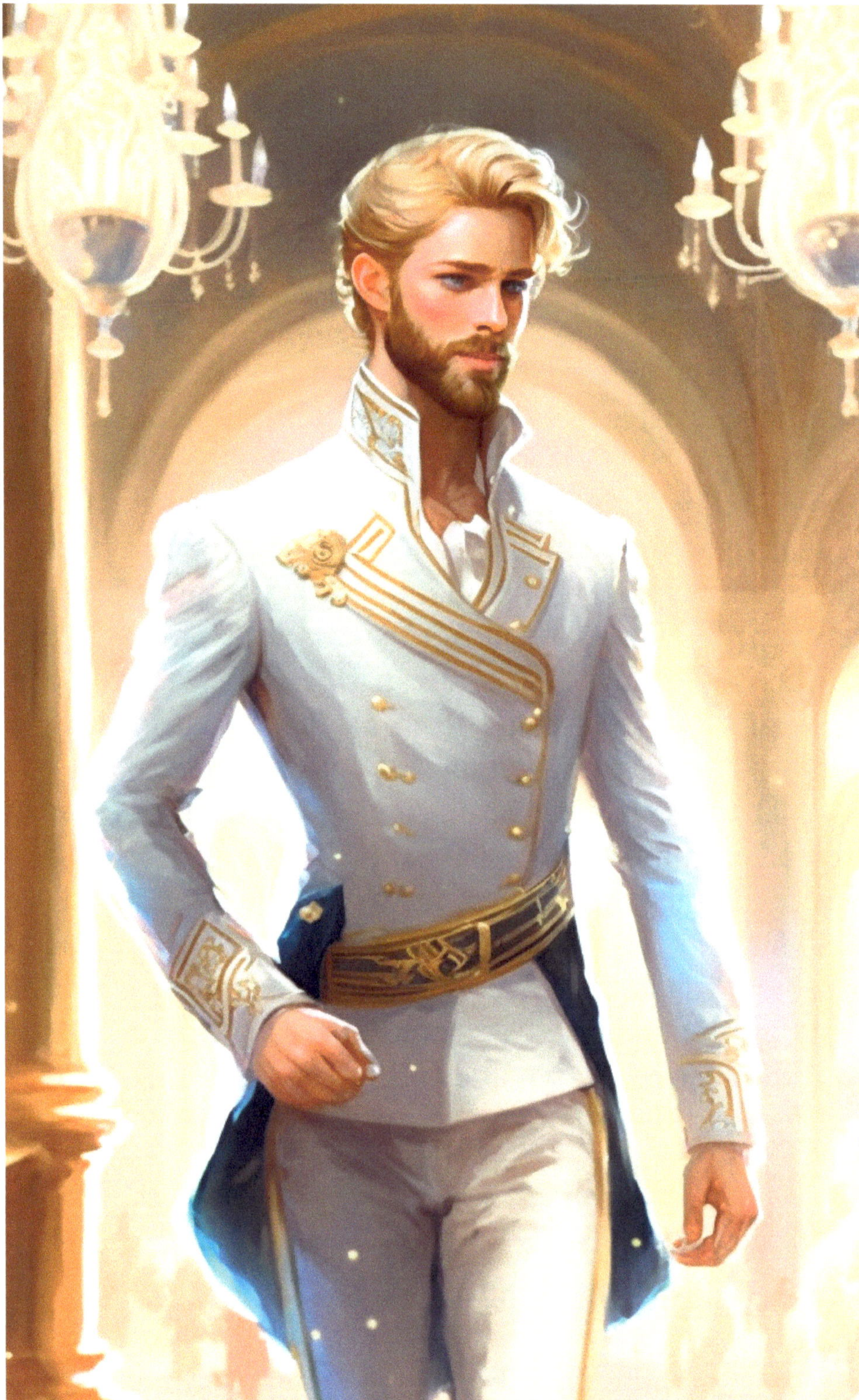

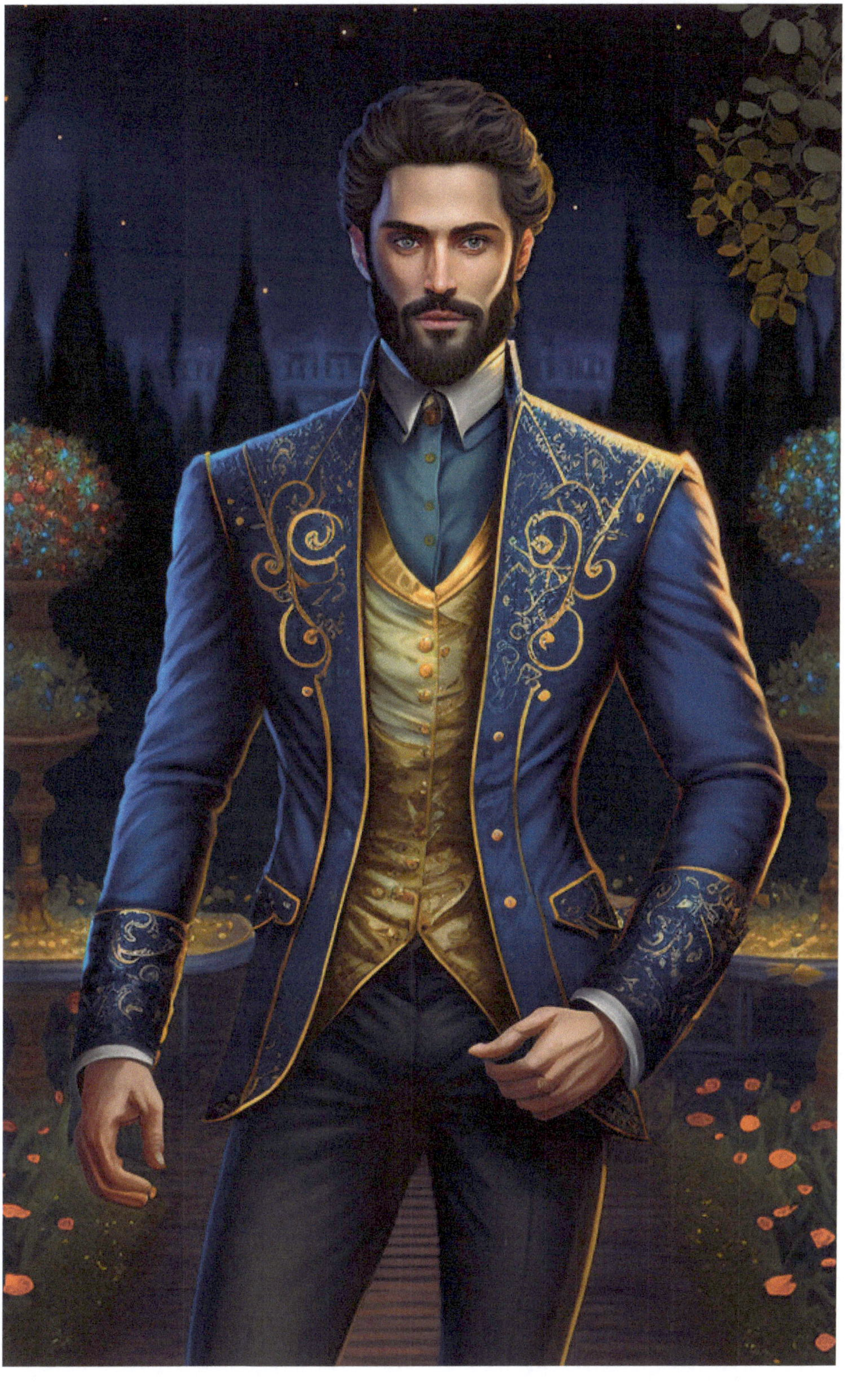

along with the king and othis nobles, dukes and archdukes who wanted the Princ Sebastian e to notice even for a second the shoes they were wearing. He got a rumor that he should see that man in glass slippers. He didn't know if it was a rumor or just a press joke. *Who could wear such shoes?* Unless he had perfect, delicate feet to walk on. And besides, they would be very pretty if he went around showing them off all over the palace. To tell the truth, it sounded tempting to see it and the Prince hoped that it was true. But he again believed that it was surely the media who spread the gossip to feed the fame of the Ball for the next day's press headlines.

Cinderello came to the garden. He walked slowly through its ivy-wrapped arches and small lights that looked like stars. It really did feel like spring on a May evening with so many lights illuminating a venue. The temperature was perfect, and the smell of roses, magnolias, and hazelnut trees were taking him to a point whise more people gathised. He had been thinking about Salvador for a long time, the man he met in the shop window to find out if he was the one who helped her friend Daniel to go to the Royal Ball. He wanted Salvador to meet him and see him dressed in that suit and be able to thank that handsome man for the help. Perhaps he was in the garden in the crowd. There in the distance, there was a man surrounded by what were possibly other men of high nobility and different importance. He couldn't see it. Possibly he was the Prince that everyone longed to see and capture their attention. Although he was curious to see him, he didn't think it was within his reach to meet him that night. There were a lot of people in the entire Royal Palace. The men around Cinderello kept watching him and whispering as he went into the garden.

People began not only to get out of his way, but to make way for him by bowing. Something strange was happening. Cinderello stopped.

The Prince was in turn surrounded when the Archduke of Alba whispered in his ear "Look, Prince Sebastian. It's true. The man with the glass shoes, there he is". Sebastian raised his head trying to see Cinderello. He made a gentle wave of his hand and everyone around him moved away to allow the Prince to focus on Cinderello.

Absolutely no one said a word. There was absolute silence. Two men like Cinderello and Prince Sebastian, had just met. The astonishment and envy of the guests did make the entire Palace fall silent. The beauty of that encounter - you could even hear the Prince's racing heart - had an entire Villa in suspense.

And it is that the guests were unaware of what was really happening. Prince Sebastian wasn't just feeling his heart racing, his hands trembling and his breathing ragged from having seen what he thought was a rumor. He also felt that a dream was coming true because the wearer of those wonderful glass loafers was nothing more and nothing less than the man he bumped into in front of the shop window. He had finally come with the suit that he achieved for him. He was unaware that the owner of the shoe store, Daniel, also kept for him such delicate and perfect jewelry for his feet for such a handsome man.

Cinderello saw that the man who was surrounded by people was approaching him. He was wearing a navy blue uniform suit with cockades and fringes on the shoulder pads that are standard for princes in royal acts. He felt confused and didn't know what to do, so he stood thise watching how he was getting closer. The formed human corridor ended at him, and that handsome man was heading towards him. And as he advanced, he learned that the very man dressed as the prince himself was actually the man he had bumped into in front of the shop window. The surprise could not be greater. He couldn't be more surprised, happy, immensely glad that the Prince was walking directly towards him.

 At that moment, the entire audience made a wide circle around them. The lights of the Grand Garden changed to something more intimate and the music of the orchestra that was at the end began to play. As the sweet waltz began to play, Cinderello was carried away by what he thought was the most handsome man in the world. Although he didn't know him - only from what the press said, and above all, from his fixation on men's feet and his shoe collection - he felt that his face and manner reflected a virtuous person.

 As they danced, he watched his eyes, large and green, and his thick, defined brows. His dark hair was long and very wavy, reaching almost to his shoulders. His beard gave off a scent of cedar and patchouli that affirmed his masculinity. His shoulders, on which Cinderello rested a hand for the dance, were hard and firm, as was the biceps on which he rested his left arm. It was noticeable that his body, which moved with confidence, was strong and agile due to the hours of training and sports. He possessed a balanced strength that perfectly controlled every step he was taking with his feet. His big feet - it was true what they said about the size of his feet-still moved with

63

ease and created their own language that matched perfectly with the delicate movement of his feet in the glass loafers. They were clad in tasseled shoes of shiny leather, furthermore ultra sheer socks so thin they looked like his own skin. It's as if the Prince's feet and Cinderello's feet were also meeting for the first time.

Prince Sebastian, in turn, also felt that he was facing the most wonderful being on Earth. It was as if all the prayers to the stars had been fulfilled. If he was already speechless when he met Cinderello that afternoon in front of the shop window, now that he had him in his arms, he felt like the luckiest man in the world. He didn't dare look at his glass loafers, but the couple of times he glanced at them, he had to look away as he felt a passion inside him grow instantly.

The music ended and the audience applauded the dancers. They both greeted and looked at each other with fear that this magical moment under the stars would not happen again. The orchestra played another waltz again, this time livelier, and the guests began to dance.

"Glad you came, Cinderello" Sebastian called him that with a certain sarcastic air, remembering his first meeting.

"The pleasure is mine, Salvador. Or I should say, your Highness, Prince Sebastian" Cinderello bowed gracely as the protocol requested.

Cinderello smiled and accepted Sebastian's arm. The masks had fallen and they already knew the identity of each one. And now it was his time to meet. Needless to say, they both wanted a little more privacy for this big meeting and headed inside the Palace, leaving the bustle and the perfumes of the Gran Garden behind.

Towards Midnight

They greeted counts, dukes and other princes, as well as important figures such as artists, fashion designers, and othis men who were stunned by the beauty and splendor of Cinderello, and the happiness that Sebastian radiated at that moment.

Cinderello was able to see his stepbrothers and his stepfather from afar, but at the moment they seemed to meet their eyes, they, as Daniel assured him, did not recognize him. Vachel only stared at his glass loafers with the violent envy so recognizable in him. But Cinderello did not think of them. He was enjoying that moment with Sebastian so much that it seemed like time had stopped.

Cinderello discovered that the Prince was a man with a sense of humor, humble, - he always thought that handsome men, especially if they were royalty, would be vain - as well as a good conversationalist. He was a lover of classical culture - a subject that both of them were passionate about - and of travel, gastronomy and philosophy. Cinderello and Prince Sebastian had toured many rooms in the Palace: the Throne room, the Armory, the impressive Gasparini Room, and other smaller spots but no less delicious places, such as the Hall of Mirrors, where they stopped.

It was the most intimate room they could find since there was no one who could interrupt them. Its mirrored walls were framed by decorated golden columns that blended with the benches where the lovers sat. The room had three large balconies that overlooked the Grand Garden from which the soft sound of the noise came. There, sitting on the velvety Prussian blue bench in the Hall of Mirrors, they couldn't stop talking about them.

Sebastian felt that this mysterious man who called himself Cinderello - he still did not know his name, but of all the times he named him, he always did it as "Cinderello" in an affectionate way - was the one he was always looking for all his life. He was a man very easy to feel comfortable with and very trustful, with a critical sense of all the topics they were talking about. And besides, of all the times he secretly diverted his gaze to his shoes, he could see his feet, the small and perfect feet of him that he glimpsed through the glass. *Was it real glass? How was it possible to walk in such shoes? How is it possible that at every step they enhanced the beauty of that part of the body that so eroticized him?* He needed to know and be closer to his feet but he didn't know how to do it.

Both were still talking, holding a glass of champagne that they took from one of the rooms where *canapés* were served. They didn't eat much since the conversation and the walk took away their hunger. But there in the Hall of Mirrors, sitting on the bench, one of the ornaments on Cinderello's shoe mask reflected the brightness of an object in the room, producing sparks that distracted both of their attention. Cinderello was about to take off his left shoe so it wouldn't reflect, but Sebastian stepped forward and knelt in front of him.

"Let me, I'll take it from you" at last the Prince found and excuse to kneel down to his feet.

Cinderello knew that Prince Sebastian was the greatest foot and shoe fetishist in the kingdom and in the Villa, but he did not imagine that he would take advantage of that moment to be at his feet and that turned him on so soon. Cinderello blushed a little, but he relaxed at the thought of how lucky he was at that moment. A moment that all the men of the Villa wanted to live, and it was to have the Prince at his feet. Cinderello let the Prince take his ankle with his left hand, and with the othis, he began to slowly remove the shoe from the heel.

"It seems that it is going to break" the Prince mumbled trembling.

The Prince watched the glass shoe holding it in his right hand, turning it around, watching it reflect and sparkle across the entire room. While he with the other hand he still held the foot "It's a real gem" he said.

"Yes, it shines bright as a diamond" replied Cinderello.

"No. I mean your foot. It is soft, with uniform and perfect color. Your fingers fall into a perfect drawing. It is narrow, elegant. A normal foot would be difficult to fit your shoe" the Prince bent down and while he was holding the foot with both hands he kissed the bridge.

"Thank you" Cinderello blushed and smiled while the Prince enjoyed his foot, which he had described as a valuable jewel.

"I want us to celebrate this meeting in a special way" said the prince, very affectionately looking at Cinderello, still kneeling down and caressing his bare foot.

"But how?"

The Prince picked up his glass of champagne and poured what was left into the small glass loafer.

"Drinking champagne, like the winners of ancient Rome. For tonight, because two very special people just met".

Cinderello was moved by such an original act and such sincere words.

The Prince picked up the glass shoe and drank all the champagne that he had poured into it. He got up and gently, holding his face caressing Cinderello's cheek, kissed him tenderly. They both felt the heat and moisture of their mouths, their tongues meeting and their beards brushing against their skins. The Prince took his foot again and delicately put the tiny glass loafer on it.

"It is very mesmerizing to see how your foot fits perfectly. I admit I'm a little excited" said the Prince while he looked at the bulge of his pants.

Cinderello laughed and put his foot on the prince's bulge feel it. The Prince smiled at the first intimate sexual act they had that night. He looked at the foot in the shoe and caressed the bridge gently. He stopped his gaze on the gold trim on the mask. It seemed like two hands on a clock striking almost twelve.

"Why do your shoes have a gold hands of a clock?"

DONG!

Cinderello's eyes widened as if he had woken up from a bad dream and he sat up instantly.
"What time is it?" asked Cinderello very worried.
"Why? Is something wrong?" - the Prince asked confused.

DONG!

The first chime of the Royal Palace rang. The Prince leaned out of the window to see the time on the clock in the Grand Garden.

"It is twelve o'clock".

DONG!

But when Sebastian turned Cinderello was gone. He had run away. He went looking for him. He couldn't believe that Cinderello had left him like this. Maybe he had a reason. Name. He went after him because he had to know his real name! *Where does he live? How could he find him?*

DONG!

The fourth bell struck and Cinderello ran through long corridors and rooms without knowing where he was. Everyone was looking at him, even some man wanted to hold him back to be able to talk to him for a moment. But he should not stop running!

DONG!

The Prince continued in his search, he did not know where he had gone. So he went to the only place whise it would be safest: the main entrance with the final brief staircase.

DONG!

Cinderello ran and ran. Daniel told him that his stepbrothers and his stepfather's spell only lasted until twelve, and he couldn't risk them knowing he was there.

DONG!

Sebastian felt desperate, it was the first time he felt that the opportunity of his life was slipping away and he was not willing to lose it.

DONG!

Cinderello felt that the sweet sweat from his feet made his shoes slippery. He arrived in the hall and had not seen his stepbrothers or his stepfather. Good! At last he saw the main exit in the distance. He had to get through the door before the last chime. He wanted to run more but if he did his shoes would come off his feet, especially his right one. He walked through the hall to the main exit. All the men present thise quickly made way for him.

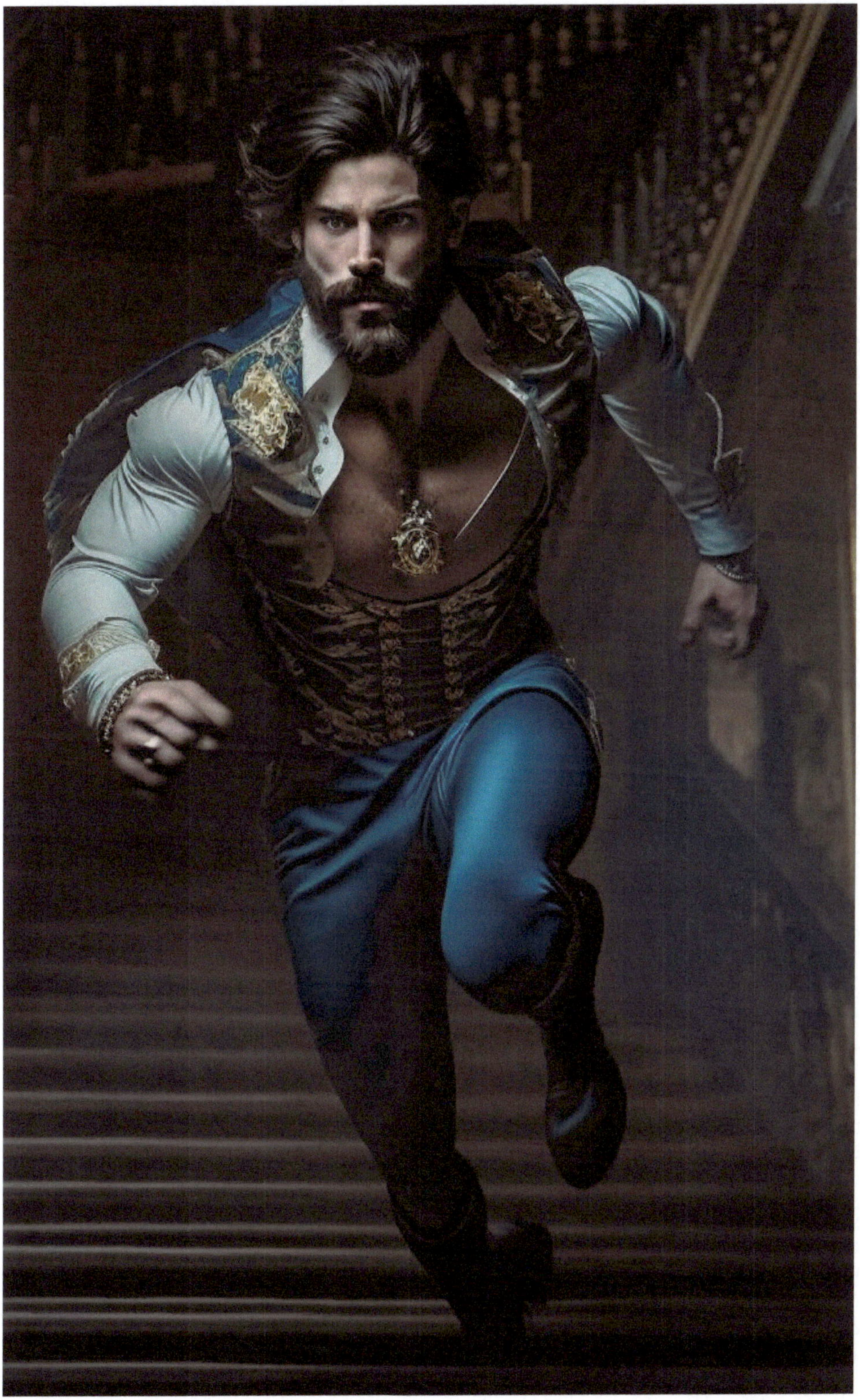

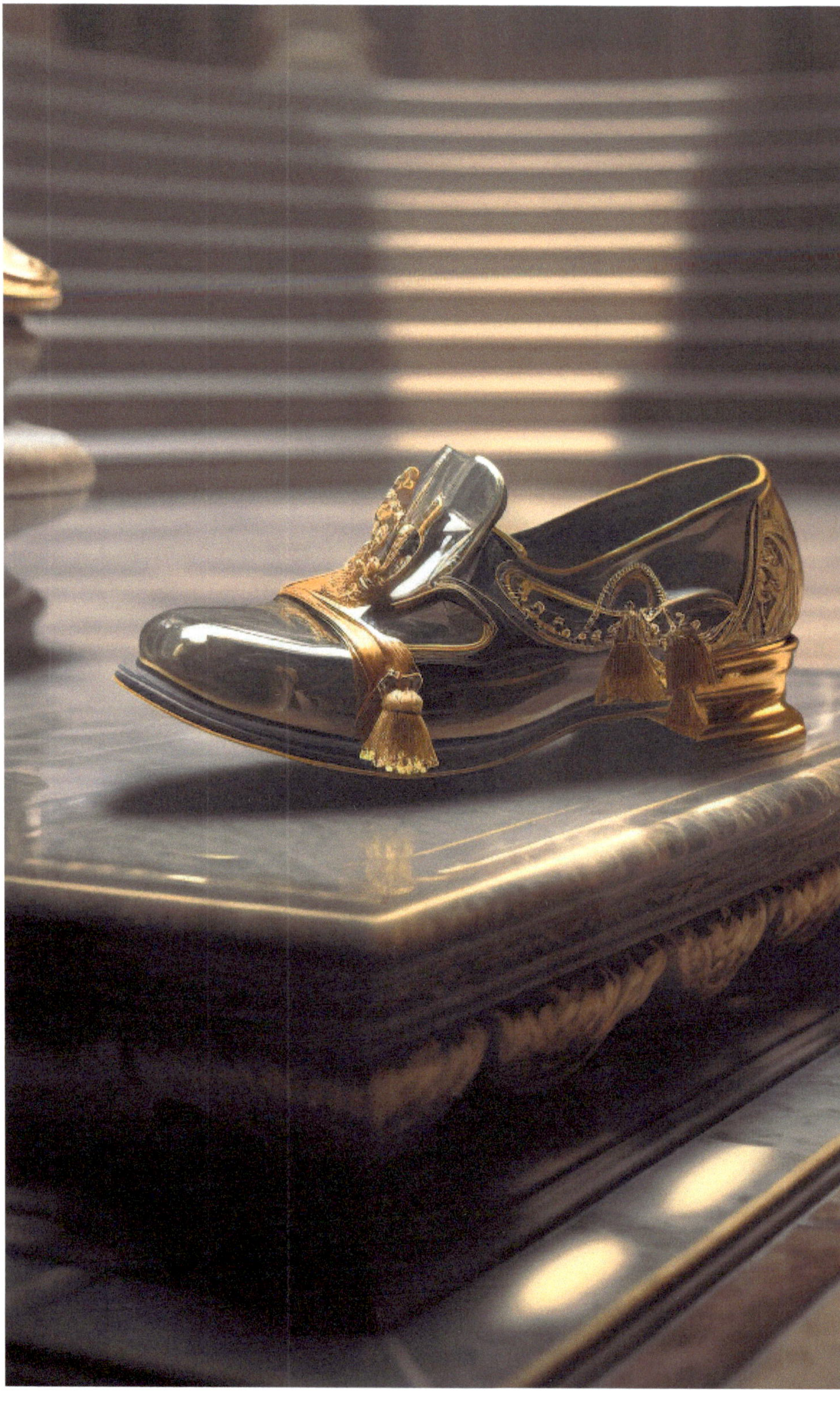

DONG!

The Prince came to the Royal Hall. He stopped for a moment to look around. Everyone in front of him was moving away from him. And suddenly, he saw Cinderello from afar, almost about to reach the main exit.

DONG!

Cinderello reached the threshold of the exit door to finally go outside towards the *Plaza de Oriente* whise his car was waiting for him at the end of the door steps.

"Wait, please, wait!" - yelled the Prince

All the men in the hall were stunned to see the Prince running and shouting, losing the manners of protocol chasing that handsome man with the glass shoes.

DONG!

Cinderello made to stop but he couldn't. Only one chime left! He did the only thing he could and that was to run more. And outside, after passing the threshold, while he listened to the Prince desperately shouting to him, he went down the few steps of the staircase. But this time he couldn't stop and the right small glass loafer from his foot felt completely off. He couldn't turn and pick it up, there was no time. He quickly got into the car.

DONG!...

The Prince saw how the glass shoe came off his beautiful foot, exposing Cinderello's beautiful sole with each step he took. The Prince stopped, hardly breating, in front of the shoe left on the stairs as he watched the car drive away with Cinderello inside. The Prince bent down and slowly picked up the glass loafer with both hands. He sat down to rest on the steps as a crowd murmured behind him. He held the glass slipper in his hands, with the saddest face a Prince had ever put on. He did not know what to do. He got up, and tucked the dainty little shoe into his jacket.

Tomorrow he would decide how to find the man of his life.

The Lost Glass Loafer

Cinderello got out of the Mercedes with only a glass slipper on his foot. He entered the house and took off the remaining shoe on his left foot so he could quickly run to the attic where he used to sleep. He took off his suit jacket and covered himself with ashes in case his step brothers came back soon and so he didn't arouse any suspicion. He kept the glass loafer that was left on his left foot safely tucked away in the closet. The other shoe was owned by Prince Sebastian. That man who had conquered him that night. He still couldn't get over his astonishment that that handsome man in the shop window was actually Prince Sebastian. Of all the men who attended the dance, he noticed him.

He looked out the small window of his attic, seeing how the Palace and the Cathedral that was next to him glowed. He could still hear the muttering of the men who were still there. He didn't want to go to bed yet, it was too early to sink into another dream that wouldn't be better than the one he had just experienced.

In turn, Prince Sebastian was left very sad and devastated and went in search of solitude, crossing as little as possible the rooms that were still crowded with guests. Although it was inevitable that some attendees would see him, he walked dejectedly through the rooms with the glass sshoe in his pocket. His father the King saw him, but he understood his grief and did not want to interrupt him until the next day.

Sebastian arrived at his room and went into the room wherehe had his shoe collection. He delicately took Cinderello's glass loafer out of his right pocket, to put it on the desk table. He sat watching him sitting in the leather chair. He caught it with both hands. He looked at it, and he could still remember that beautifully-toned foot, with perfect toes, with tendons that stood out as if they had been sculpted in ancient Greece, and the narrowness of the perfect foot for an equally narrow shoe. His bridge and his soles, oh, his beautiful soles that he remembered from the moment Cinderello lost his glass loafer.

He could tell that the missing shoe was still warm inside. He brought his face closer and inhaled deeply the smell of Cinderello's foot soaked in the moisture that emanated from the moccasin. He smelled of him, he smelled of Cinderello, of that man with an unknown name. He noticed the warm scent in his nose and noticed that there was still a drop of sweat on the edge of the heel. He ran his finger around to scoop up the drop and sucked on it as if it were royal jelly. He inhaled again and couldn't

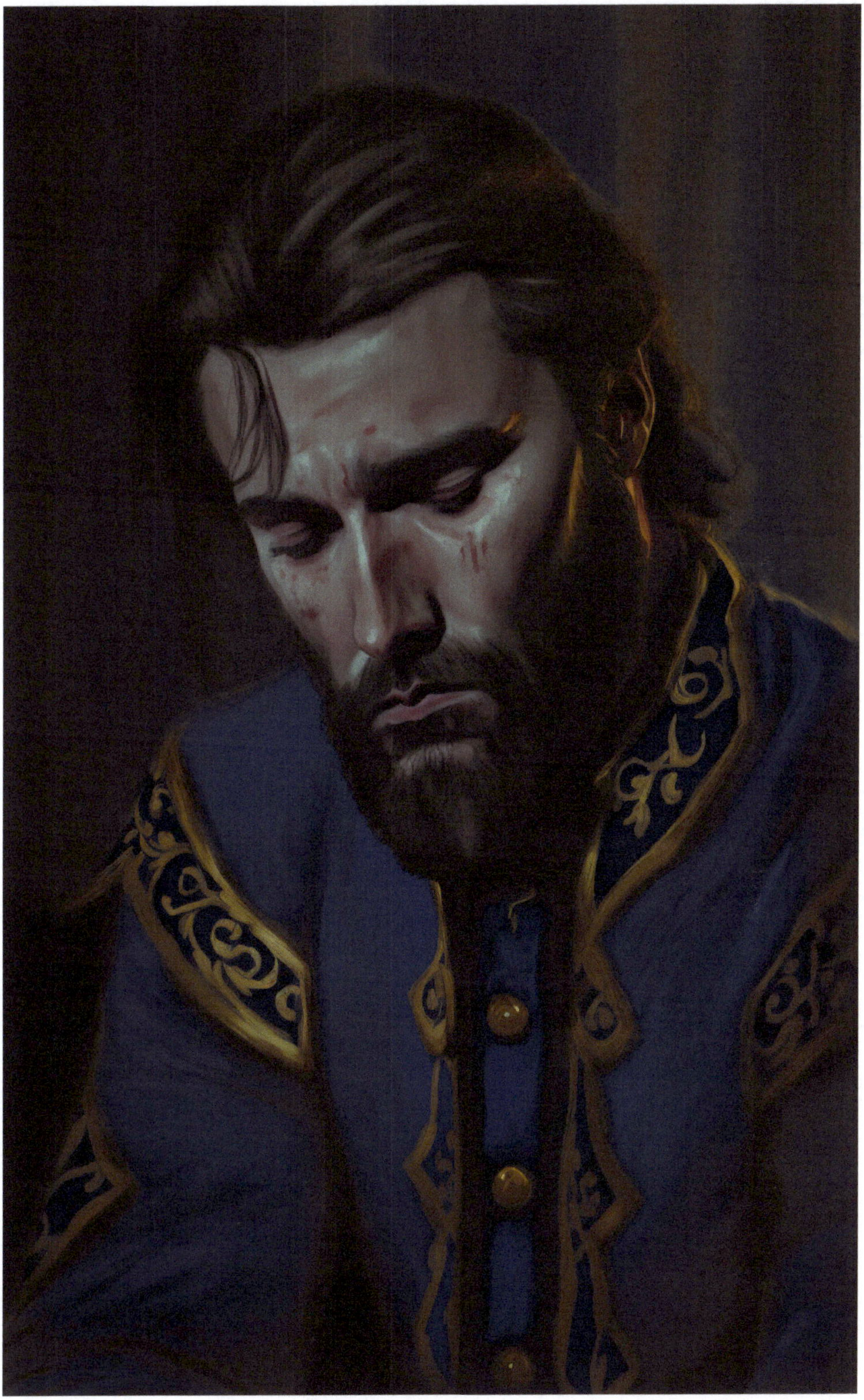

help but get hard. He couldn't take it anymore, he was excited to know that he had found the man of his dreams and that he had perfect feet in shape, smell, size and touch. His cock began to leak pre-cum. It was so much that he instantly pierced his pants. He didn't resist and pulled out his cock to touch it for the first time with that jewel that had touched such a beautiful foot. He was afraid of breaking it, but his arousal was such that he put his cock inside the shoe. He still felt tempered, which allowed him to imagine everything he wanted to do with Cinderello. He began to masturbate with the shoe, putting his whole cock inside it, up to the toe. He felt that he was corrupting such a precious piece and that he was not worthy of touching it. However, instantly he noticed his torrent of semen that filled the entire tip of the shoe. Pulling his cock out of him, the last drops of his milk joined the beads of sweat from Cinderello's foot.

While he rested in the chair, lightly hugging the shoe, he found himself with the strength to do the impossible to find it. He could ask the owner of the shoe store, but neither the Prince nor any member of royalty could by law enter the houses unless he had a license. And those permits took about two months to process. In that case he would have to come up with a way for Cinderello to go to the Palace. Therefore he devised the following: he would proclaim that all those attending the Spring Ball would come to the palace to try on the crystal loafer. As the owner of the shoe store explained to him, that shoe and the pair of it were unique, made to measure. And he, being a specialist in shoes and feet, being the greatest fetishist man in the Kingdom, could assure that it was a shoe that could only suit a man with a specific foot; just a shape - with not much instep - , the size - small but not too much, an unusual size without being ridiculously small, and misshapen -, and the touch - a softer than normal to allow slipping at first, and in turn, detach-.

Thus, he ordered the following day that that same week all attendees had the obligation to go to the Royal Palace to try on the glass shoe lost by a man at the stroke of midnight. He himself would supervise the fitting - along with his faithful assistant Niels - so as not to receive any deceit and to be able to test it in person to Cinderello. Thus he announced himself by all means, in turn sending a written order to every house, just as he did with the invitation to the dance. There was no time to lose.

XIII
The Fitting of the Glass Shoe in the Royal Palace

And so the Prince and his messenger began their search for the rightful owner of the glass slipper. It had only been a couple of days and Vachel and Crispin were the first to come. As soon as Cinderello's stepfather found out that the prince had ordered that all attendees were obliged to try on the shoe, he preferred to stay at home to keep an eye on Cinderello. He couldn't risk him escaping to try on the shoe. In any case, he had the feeling that one of his sons would fit the glass loafer perfectly, most certainly, but even so, he did not want to take risks by leaving there.

So he once again entrusted him with tasks that would tire and lower Cinderello's spirits. In any case, he already warned him "The glass slipper is supposedly very tiny. The men who have come to the first shift in the morning have already spread the word about how impossible it is to put your foot in. Since you didn't come, Cinderello, now that my sons are leaving, you can take the opportunity to clean their rooms thoroughly. In any case, you have no hope, surely one of my little men will be able to fit the lost loafer".

Vachel and Crispin were greatly relieved at the Palace knowing that Cinderello had no chance of trying on the lost shoe. Crispin was absolutely certain that he could fit that glass slipper. When he saw the man wearing them from afar at the Ball he could tell that it was exactly his size. The owner of the shoe had not yet put on the shoe and no one had yet. Vachel did not even consider that it was his size. He just knew he was going to fit it in, since with a little effort he would surely fit. His big feet were sure to charm the Prince, because he sure liked the feet of men as big as the ones the Prince had.

Meanwhile, Sebastian was taking turns with his footman Niels to try on the shoe in every eligible man. Of all the servants and footmen that could help him, he knew that Niels was the one since he enjoyed being close to men's feet just as much as he did. He also did it in a very particular way: if the foot was big, he used to take the shoe with both hands, waiting to receive the foot. Since the big feet were very heavy, he couldn't pick it up and push with one hand. On the contrary, with small feet he used to let the man support his small foot in his hand, thus completely brushing the sole of his foot.

The shoe fitting procedure was determined as follows: each man was allowed three minutes to try on the delicate crystal loafer. That without counting the moment before previously going through supervision so that his

83

feet were cleaned in case they were dirty, he had to do a quick pedicure or simply say that they were not presentable for the prince because they were too ugly. In this case, which were quite a few, many men burst into tears. Some others claimed that this was the shoe he had lost that night.

He started the afternoon shift and this time it was Prince Sebastian's turn to kneel in the throne room in front of the red velvet chair where the suitors sat. An archduke he did not know arrived. He was a handsome grown man, somewhat graying, nearing fifty but his care had not aged him. He brought his foot closer to Sebastian's so he caught him by the ankle. Sebastian began to approach carefully, until he inserted all five toes into the small glass loafer.

His fingers began to tighten inside the glass, but still, the Prince thought, he might have a chance. *Could he have been the owner?* Who knows what can change a person overnight. There came a time when the Prince, as he helped to push the foot, the Archduke emitted a slight moan. It was clear that he was already starting to bother him and pinch the shoe. Yet it was now the Archduke who was pushing anyway towards the end of the shoe, wanting it to go all the way in. The Archduke writhed and pushed with no chance of getting anothis millimeter behind him. About an inch of the heel was yet to go in but the prince stopped him. He couldn't risk the effort of the suitors cracking the shoe.

"No, sorry, it doesn't fit. Next!" The Prince was already beginning to be tired, but he felt that sooner or later Cinderello would arrive and fit his lost shoe.

The next one he sat down was a fairly young guy,

about twenty-five years old. He sat down nervously. He was average. All these men were trying on a shoe that they knew was not theirs but that they had a chance of being with the prince if they did wear it. The prince himself had promised it in the order that he had sent to all means:

"That man, who, without conditions, manages to put on the missing glass slipper at midnight of the Spring Ball <u>without any effort</u>, will be the Consort Prince of Prince Sebastian."

The boy who sat down, although he had already gone through supervision, took off the Stan Smith sneaker that he was wearing. Sebastian saw that his foot, though not very pretty, certainly if it was small. Although not enough. So he tried. The boy began to insert the five toes of his right foot, smoothly, without problem. The truth is that Sebastián noticed that his heart was racing. Could it be that Cinderello boy? He could look like him if he changed his hairstyle. He couldn't know until he fully slipped on the glass slipper. The boy pushed a little more and when he almost had his heel in, he saw that his heel was a bit thick and it didn't fit at first, however, he made a little effort and pushed, and finally, his foot clicked into the glass shoe.

All attendees were amazed. Some of them even began to cry since someone had finally managed to put on the crystal moccasin. Sebastian frozed. He didn't know how to react. However, thise was something weird in that vision of that foot into the glass shoe. He began to see how the heel reddened. He looked at the boy's face, who was trying to hide a little discomfort. Until he screamed:

"Take it off me please, it hurts! It hurts so much!"

Sebastian quickly took it off, trying not to break it, and stormed out of the throne room angrily. He didn't tolerate them trying on the shoe with that impudence! They could break it and all their hope of finding Cinderello would be dashed!

He decided to continue but this time he would not allow something like that. At the slightest that the shoe did not fit, he would disqualify the suitor.

Throughout that afternoon thise was a succession of all kinds of feet: large, even very small but wide and deformed, medium, pretty (but not as many as Cinderello's), and ugly (despite this, they were also forced to try it on).

Vachel and Crispin were finally able to try it at around seven in the evening. However, the Prince was not there on that shift, but his assistant Niels. When Vachel first sat down in the chair, knowing that this shoe was for him, he realized that not even all five of his toes could fit. At that point he got angry and insulted Niels, which got him immediately kicked out of the Throne Room.

Crispin later tried on the shoe, but to no avail. He didn't manage to slide his foot in as besides having a wide foot, it wasn't as soft as Cinderello's. Despite the many ointments and good treatments they received from Cinderello, his feet didn't last even two seconds in the shoe. Vachel was so angry that he blamed Cinderello and he was going to pay for it as soon as he got home. Crisipín was sad, he was very convinced that he was going to be able to put the shoe on, and inside he knew that his feet were not perfect like Cinderello's, who, if he were to try it on, knew that he could possibly put it on even if it wasn't his.

The two stepbrothers left the Palace very disappointed, although relieved because they knew that Cinderello, by not going to the dance, could not try on the shoe. They were both very secretly envious of his feet and knew that he had a good chance of wearing it. If he ever had the chance to prove it, they would do everything possible to stop him.

XIV
This Glass Shoe is Impossible to Fit In!

Exactly one month passed and none of the attendees who responded to the call to the Royal Palace failed to perfectly fit the lost glass shoe. All the men in the Villa looked devastated for not having been able to put on that small shoe. It was unheard of that they couldn't if they themselves saw the man who accompanied the Prince at the Royal Ball take them. Therefore it must be possible. And the owner of the other pair had not even come, therefore it is likely that everything was a montage by the press, which spent several days talking about the impossible-to-fit glass loafer. They wondered how it was so. The confusion was too great even for the Prince, even coming to think that it was all a hoax.

Sebastian was devastated. He didn't feel like eating or sleeping. However, his father the King reminded him that there was still hope with the possibility of going from house to house with the shoe repeating the fitting, since it could be the case that not all those attending the first test there in the Palace had come for whatever reason they were unaware of. Sebastian and the King knew that it was a rather tedious system, since it would take about six months to get legal permission to enter the houses. Even if there was such a long shot, Sebastian was willing to wait to find the owner of the glass slipper, his Cinderello.

Thus, as the months passed, the gay men of the Villa forgot so unpleasant matter of the glass shoe. The feeling that was generated in those moments of uncertainty, and anger - for not being able to put it on -, plunged the Villa into sadness. But Cinderello's sadness did not come from the same situation, but from not being able to see again the only man who really fit into his heart and who still had his other shoe. He had thought of ways to go to the Palace with the shoe and present himself there, but the surveillance, as always, was very strict, and the impossibility of dressing properly would make them take him for a madman. In addition, his stepfather kept him under strict surveillance because he blamed his for the fact that none of his "little men" could have fitted the glass slipper. So it was almost impossible to leave the house.

But after six months, it was announced again that Prince Sebastian was going to repeat the fitting of the lost glass shoe, so it was demanded that all those who received notification that the Prince and his messenger Niels were going to go to his house to the shoe test, their feet were strictly clean and presentable. In addition, the prince planned to try the shoe even on those men he saw fit, who even without having gone to the Ball, had possibilities.

Therefore, this time, every day for four hours, Cinderello was ordered by his stepfather to care for, clean, rub, and massage the feet of not only his step brothers, but also his stepfather, who was determined to try on the glass loafer too.

 So Sebastian went from house to house, going up and down the stairs of buildings, using elevators, entering homes and offices, trying the shoe again on men of all kinds who appeared on his list who had attended and not only that, even those who had not attended and wanted to try it on; of all sexual orientation -even straight men wanted desperately to try on the glass loafer, even if he had to marry the Prince- and ages from sixteen to seventy. But absolutely no foot could fit. Most of them had trouble getting all five toes in, and those who did couldn't slide their feet. And those who seemed to have the right size, -which were very few-, could not reach much further due to the instep or simply, the heel did not fit. And of course, flat feet were a given since they didn't have any curves that allowed them to slide their feet. Although having a small foot helped, it was not enough or determining. The men with big feet, knowing this, still tried it, since perhaps the shape of their feet could allow them to slide through the shoe, and by pressing a little, insert the foot all the way.

One man even cut his toes and wrapped them in tight bandages and managed to fit the small glass loafer. But when he got to his feet the pain from him was so strong that he passed out, staining his shoe with blood. This incident made the shoe try on even more under strict rules: the slightest thing that didn't seem to fit, the man who was trying on the shoe at the time was disqualified. So this made it practically impossible to fit it. The legend of the impossible-to-fit glass shoe was still alive.

It was around 6pm in November, close to sunset, when Cinderello finished removing the dead skin from the feet of Vachel and his stepfather and wrapping the feet of Vachel very tightly in some rags. Crispin, orderly but his stepfather, since he is the one who, according to him, had the best chance of putting on the shoe. He knew that the Prince would be about to arrive and he could only put on a pair of jeans that, even though they were a bit torn, fit him well, and a freshly washed white tee. At his feet he continued to wear his espadrilles. But this time he hadn't gotten his feet dirty in ash so he could get the Prince's attention and try his luck. Only those who attended the Ball were required to try on the shoe, but he had heard that those that Prince Sebastian caught his attention would also let him try it on.

The doorbell rang and his stepfather ordered Cinderello to open the door. However, Dorrel, seeing him dressed down the stairs without his usual dirty clothes, was scandalized, and threw him to the ground to drag him to the living room whise the fireplace and ashes were. Dorrel dirty not only Cinderello's feet, but his entire face.

It was quite a tense and violent moment: the doorbell started ringing and ringing, and Cinderello couldn't come as Vachel came to the call of his father to take care of him. Vachel dragged him up the stairs to his room with his strong arms.

Dorrel finally opened the main door and opened it widely.

Sebastian was received by a man who seemed conceited due to his voice and his unnatural appearance. He entered the house, weary, carrying on his arm a blue velvet cushion whise the glass loafer perched. The Prussian blue velvet cushion was surrounded by gold cord and tassels that made the shoe appear all the more shiny and delicate.

At that moment, Cinderello was listening downstairs in the hall to the voice of Sebastian and his stepfather inviting him to enter the living room. He wanted with all his might to show himself in front of the man of his dreams. He thought about meeting him many times but he never thought it was like that. Vachel was holding him so tightly and dragging him towards the attic so fast that it was impossible for him to react properly. He was practically unrecognizable, as smeared with ash as he was. By the time they reached the attic, Vachel began beating his face and body, leaving his nose bleeding and unconscious on the floor. Thus Vachel ensured that Cinderello lost any chance of trying on the glass loafer.

The Prince and his assistant Niels stood waiting when Crispin had sat down in the chair for the shoe fitting. Niels stepped forward

"I remind you that the test has to be carried out in a delicate and natural way. At the minimum act that threatens the integrity of the shoe is attempted, you will be disqualified. The shoe must be tried on in one movement".

The prince dropped to one knee in front of Crispin and he nervously stretched out his right foot wrapped in the thin sock that wrapped the tight bandages.
"The shoe must be tried on naked" said the prince.

Crispin didn't know what to do, but his stepfather ordered him to take it off "Take it off my son. Your foot will already be so shrunken and small that it will not be difficult for you to fit your shoe perfectly".

It took Crispin a while to remove his sock and bandages and the Prince began to get impatient. But when Crispin was ready and raised his foot again, this time more nervously, the Prince tried it on but could not gently insert all five fingers. The foot was still too wide.

"Next" Sebastian said.

Vachel, who violently grabbed his brother's arm and pushed him away.

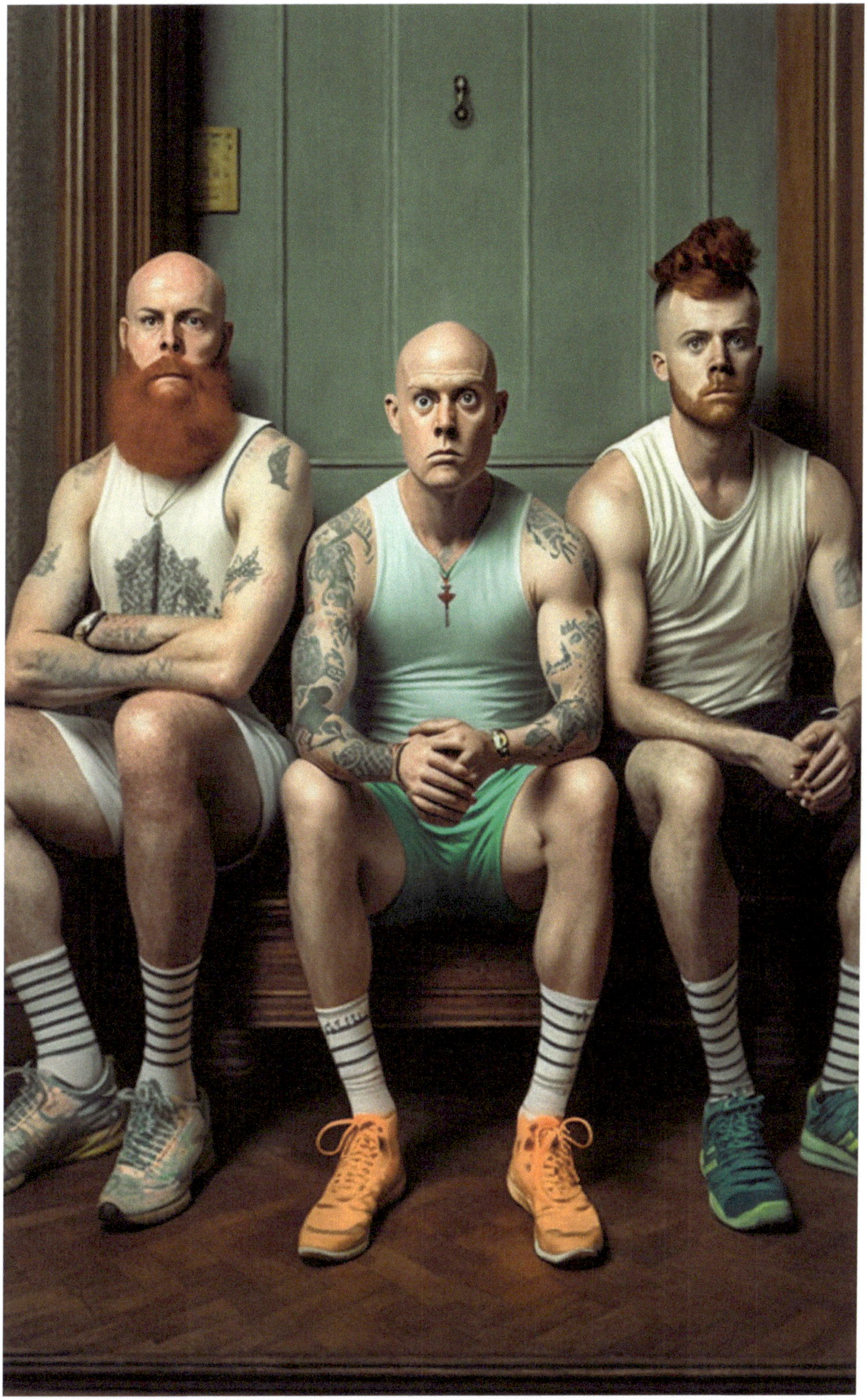

Vachel removed his size 12 Nike Airmax and began inserting himself into the small shinny glass loafer. He remembered all the times that he used Cinderello's mouth as a shoe and tried to introduce his foot. But this time it seemed that it was going to be a little more complicated. He could only insert four fingers, the little finger being outside. So he quickly pushed it into him with his hand, but the helper warned him and disqualified him.
"Oh no. Do not try it, sir. It is not your shoe. The fitting ends here".warned Niels.

Vachel rose from the chair in a rage, controlling his rage that was appeased by Dorrel. The stepfather looked at the shoe, and asked to try on the shoe, since he also attended the Ball. Seeing it fair, the Prince and his assistant allowed him to try on the shoe. Sebastian helped him remove his right shoe. It was a slightly hairy foot and what is called a square foot - he remembered that Cinderello's was Greek, with a perfect fall -. It was very shiny, maybe he was sweating, but his foot couldn't shine that much because of sweat. Sebastian brought the shoe closer to stepfather's foot, and he put all five fingers in it for the first time. However, he didn't keep sliding, making a silly movement that he hid by settling in the chair and holding on to his behind. So what he did was he took his foot out of it again, he slid it back in and the first time, he put his foot in the shoe.

Sebastian couldn't believe it, finally, possibly, he had found the owner of the small glass loafer. However, he remembered that Cinderello didn't fit it that way when he tried it on the night they met. As he demanded, the movement had to be clean, the first time. Also, he seemed to be squeezing him a bit. And he found it suspicious that the foot was so shiny. He heard a snap on the floor. Something had fallen nearby. It was a bottle of vaseline that fell out of the stepfather's pants pocket. Sebastian grabbed the stepfather by the ankle and the assistant removed the shoe from his swallowed foot instantly.

"Enough of all this deception! Vaseline to be able to fit the foot in the shoe! Fool the Prince of your Villa like this! I will order you to be prosecuted for this!" Sebastian now he was really raged and he couldn't hide it "Let's get out of this house! It's the last one left and it's clear to me now: Cinderello, the man I love never existed! This shoe has to be destroyed!"

"No my Lord, I swear it's my shoe, you saw that it fits, I also wore the vaseline at the Ball so I could dance with you all night!" Dorrel begged stupidly.

Prince Sebastian picked up the shoe and headed for the door. But at the moment when the exit door would have been opened, he heard a sound from the entrance stairs that allowed him to go to the upper floors.

"Is thise anyone else in the house?"

Dorrel, Vachel, and Crispin looked up to see Cinderello trying to crawl down, smeared with ash and blood. They tried to hide him but it was too late because the prince's messenger saw how mistreated Cinderello was.

"What are you doing, monsters?" Niels the footman struggled with the three of them.

"If you continue like this, I'll send you to jail and you know perfectly well that I have the power to do that, you fools!" The Prince shouted while he was watching that scene.

Faced with such a threat, both the stepbrothers and the stepfather stopped struggling and allowed Cinderello to crawl across the floor towards the hall. The assistant took pity on such a painful image of a man lying on the ground so dirty with ashes and his face stained with blood that he helped him get up and carry him to a place whise he could sit.

Sebastian was confused by the situation, seeing a man who, even if he was stained, was certainly attractive. While he saw how Niels helped him sit in the armchair in the living room whise the step brothers had tried on the small glass loafer, Sebastian couldn't help but approach him and kneel down to caress his face and accompany him. Cinderello was slightly dizzy and seemed to be regaining consciousness. They looked at each other. A blue glace that hadn't cast a spell on him like that for a long time.

"Who are you"? Sebastian recalled.

Cinderello could not articulate a word and at that moment he began to cry slightly. Sebastian understood that the man was a bit in shock. He looked at him sweetly.

"That is nobody, Your Highness! He is just a filthy servant!" yelled Crispin desperately.

Sebastian held up a hand to silence them. He looked at his right foot, which had lost an espadrille. He was all smeared with ash and cinders.

-Cinders... - Sebastian felt an irrepressible desire to try the glass shoe on that foot still stained with ash. It looked very pretty.

He picked up the shoe that was still resting on the cushion. With his left hand on Cinderello's heel, and with the other hand he brought the glass loafer closer. Cinderello's and Sebastian's hearts were racing, even Sebastian noticed that he had instantly wet his pants from the excitement that was being generated. And in a single movement, his five fingers began to slide and then gently covered the entire shoe until without any effort, the heel placed in the glass shoe perfectly.

At that moment, Vachel became enraged, releasing all possible insults that would not be proper to reproduce here. Crispin fell to his knees and began to weep with envy and jealousy, and Dorrel faked a faint that no one took any notice of. Only the Prince and his assistant couldn't stop looking at that perfect foot that, even stained with ash, looked beautiful perfectly fitted into the shiny glass shoe.

"It fits perfectly! I've found my prince. - said Sebastian staring at Cinderello's eyes

"Jay, my name is Jay. Thanks for saving my shoe. He is the partner of this one" Cinderello took the other glass shoe out of his pants pocket.

Prince Sebastian showed true astonishment and his eyes moistened from the beauty of such a precious moment. Cinderello offered him the smallshoe and Sebastian took it. He began to get excited and at that moment, just as the Prince began to put the shoe on him, Cinderello and the prince kissed at the same time as the heel fitted perfectly. The Prince noticed while they kissed that his cock exploded with excitement. They trembled while they kissed due to the orgasm produced by Cinderello's foot inside the shoe.

The stepbrothers saw all this and never in their lives felt such envy and jealousy as at that moment. Although they never regretted the mistreatment they caused Cinderello during all those years, they did regret all their lives for having such big and ugly feet and for never being able to have feet so perfect that a prince could fall in love.

And that's how Jay and Sebastian found each othis again and will be togethis forever. Two men who love feet and shoes, men of virtue who made the Villa very happy forever.

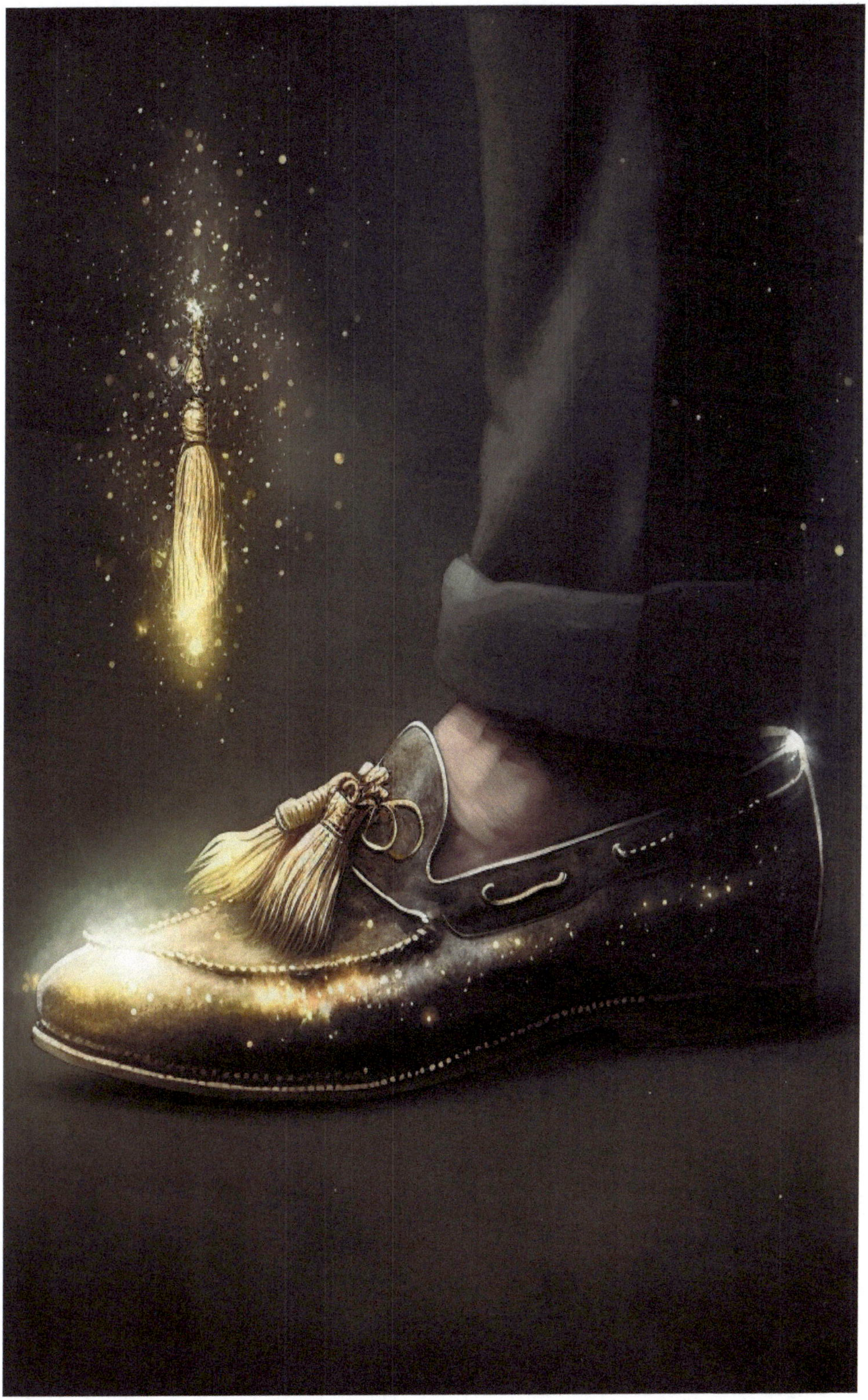

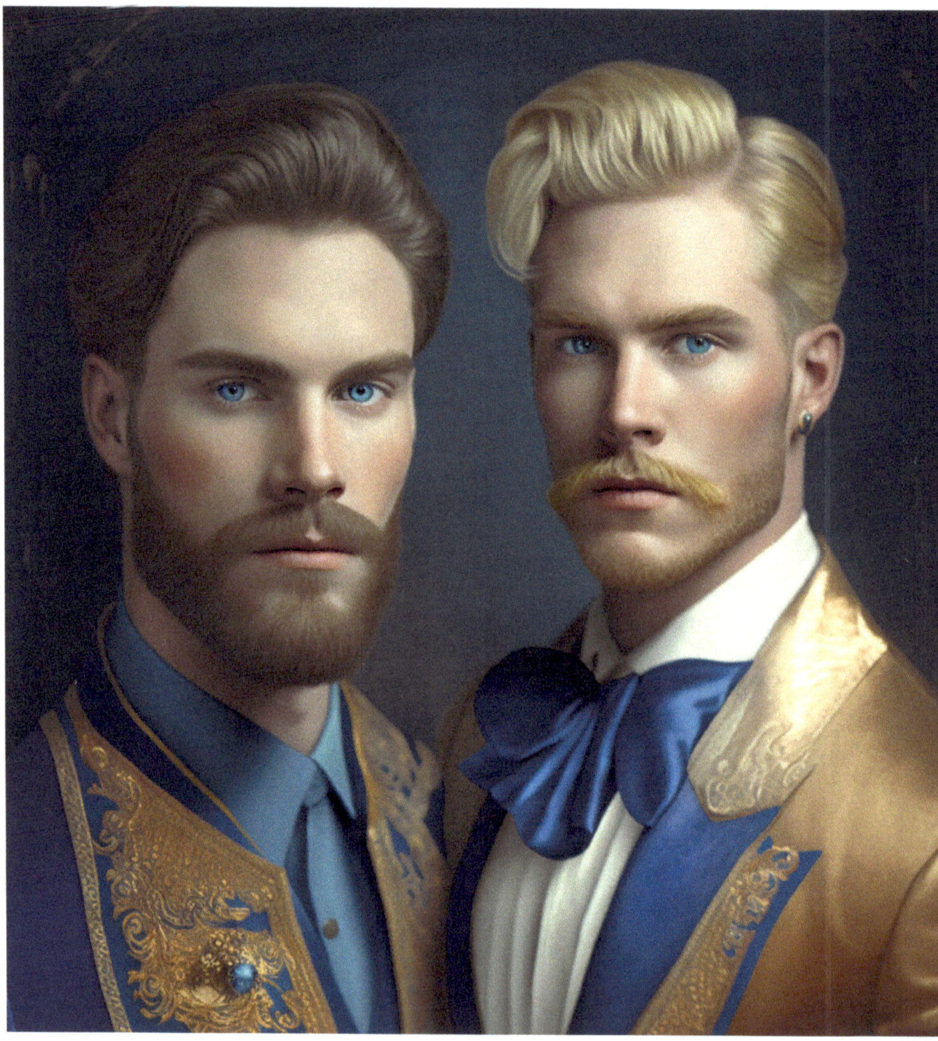

EPILOGUE
A Gift for Cinderello

It had already been a year since Sebastian and Jay met again thanks to Jay's perfect feet. Sebastian continued affectionately calling Jay on occasions, "My Cinderello", and this one, to Sebastian "My Prince". They both got very horny by calling each othis those names. Cinderello had become the Consort King of the now King Sebastian I Kingdom. They were very happy and tried to make the Villa and the Kingdom also happy and wealthy. Furthermore, every time they had sex, they fucked surrounded by Sebastian's shoes and the shoes that he gave Jay as a gift made by Daniel. His perfect feet had to be adorned with the prettiest shoes ever.

One night, as usual, Jay began massaging Sebastian's huge, beautiful feet. He couldn't resist it, they were the feet of a King and they belonged to him, they were his. So he continued to suck them, lick them, every nook and corner: the heel, the fingers, the big toe, as if it were his cock, and Sebastian loved this. So they went to the bed, where on eithis side of it were Sebastian's shoes on wooden shelves.

"Try me some shoes, the ones you want today, just like I tried them on the day I met you again".- said Sebastian.

Cinderello chose black, masked ones with a low blade (a low blade goes in easier), but Sebastian asked him please that this time they should be the ones with tassels. In addition, he asked his to take some executives from the drawer, which were blue "because I am and always will be your prince charming", -said Sebastian- made of a very, very fine fabric. They were so thin that when he knelt down to put Sebastian's blue navy *ejecutivos* sheers on, it almost felt like a second skin. For both of them, using *ejecutivos* was like putting a condom on a cock. He pulled them up to his knee. First the right foot, and then the left. He took the big tasseled loafers and brought them out on a silver tray, just the way they both liked it.

Sebastian was naked, alone with the *ejecutivos*, sitting in the velvet chair. His long, wavy brown hair was always perfect, along with his eyes and square-jawed beard.

"Try my shoes on to see if they fit me, my Cinderello. I want to continue being your prince and king, as long as you are mine".

Jay was starting to get as wet as Sebastian, his cock dripping so much that it left a trail on the blue velvet of the chair. He picked up the right shoe, and put it on. His fingers and heel slided so smoothly that he had to do it several times because of the beauty of the moment. Cin-

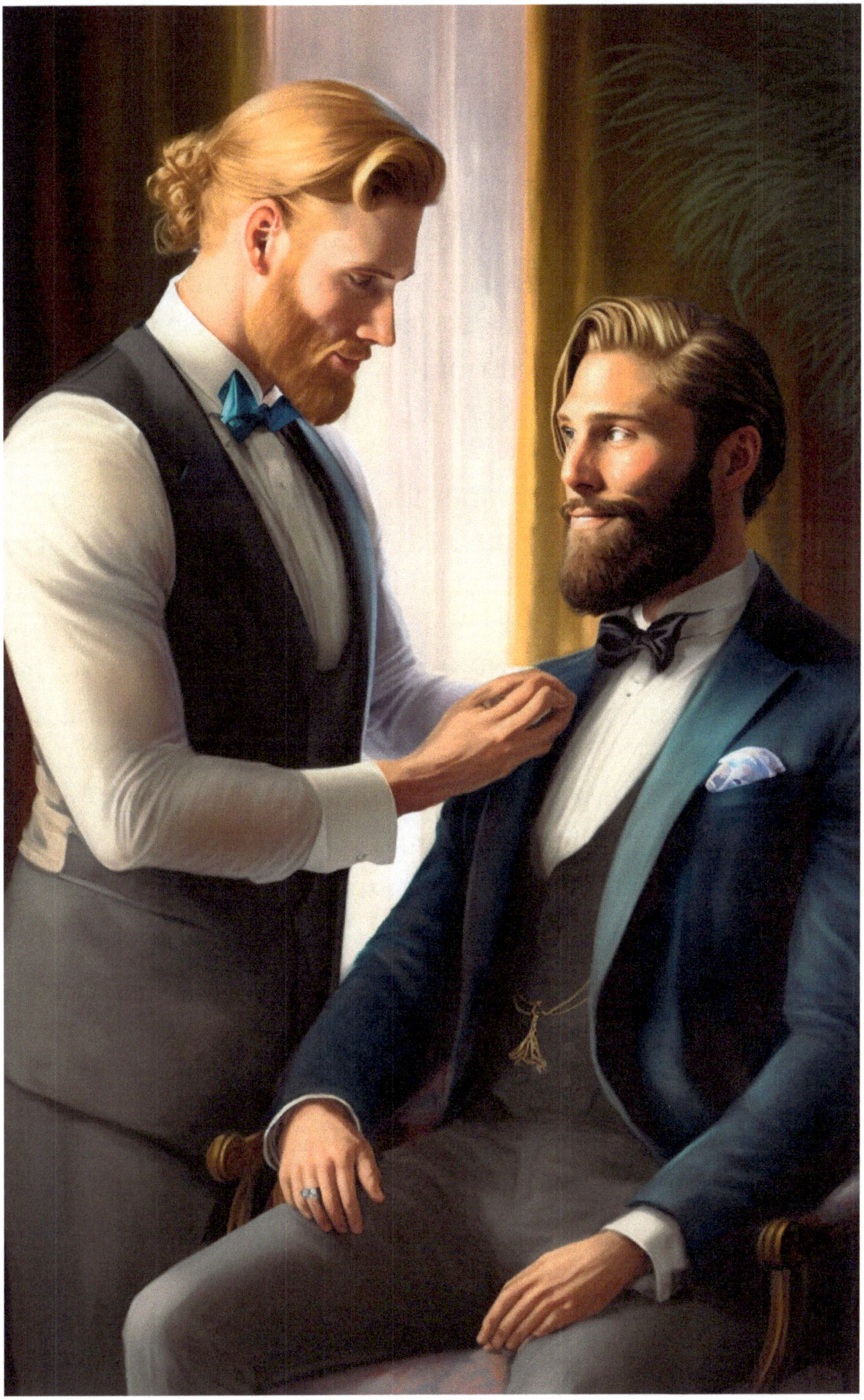

derello repeated it over and over again until Sebatian got up.

"It's time to give you your surprise, my Cinderello. Lie down on bed.

"Yes, my prince".

Jay stretched out on the bed and watched Sebastian go to the glass loafers that stood on a specially lit display case in the center of the room. However, he did not take them, but instead brought a box that he took from a drawer under the same cabinet.

"What is?"

"Be patient, my Cinderello. You will know it soon".

Sebastian gently pushed Jay to lay him down. He gently took him by the legs and began to lick his ass, preparing him as he used to. Sebastian was still wearing his *ejecutivos* and tassel loafers - Jay knew they were his favorites, and he was understanding that it was a special occasion -.

At that moment, with his very wet cock, he began to penetrate Jay. He did it gently. Getting his dick in and out of him a few times. Sebastian had to lean a little with each movement, and his heels stuck out of his huge shoes a little thanks to the softness of the *ejecutivos* sheer socks. But there was an instant that he stopped and stayed inside him, and jay felt his cock throb. Sebastian turned behind him, trying not to get out of Jay. He opened the box and took out a small glass sloafer with golden tassels. It was even prettier than the ones he wore to the Royal Ball, if that was possible. They both felt their hearts race.

"I don't know if it's your size".

Jay was very, very nervous. Sebastian began to put on his right foot. His shoe slipped off the in just one movement.

"Yeah, it fits perfectly. -Sebastian said, trembling.

"Try the othis one to see. I'm not sure it's my shoe".

They both smiled at this comment. At that moment Cinderello noticed for the first time how much Sebastian's cock could swell. His prince's cock, who conquered him for his perfect feet.

"There's only one way to make sure it fits perfectly too, my Cinderello".

Sebastian, before putting on the other shoe, began to lick Jay's foot. He spent fifteen minutes licking that perfect foot in every possible way. Sebastian, in turn, wouldn't take his cock out of Jay's ass, so that he would feel how horny it made him to be able to eat his feet like that.

He very easily put all five fingers in his mouth, very, very deep into his mouth. When he saw that his entire foot was dripping with saliva, he picked up the glass shoe and brought it closer to Jay's foot. They both listened to how the gold tassels tinkled along with the sound of saliva helping to slide the foot. Jay knew that with those shoes they both felt complete, they were the Sebastian's favorite shoes and even more, they could wear them while they made love and Sebastian could see the soles of his feet while he penetrated his.

At that moment, Jay was so excited that he asked Sebastian to fuck him. The prince got so turned on by this request, along with the fact that he could see his perfect feet through the glass, that he didn't stop going in and out of his ass. Due to the sweat the right shoe almost slipped off Jay's foot, and that's when their arousal began to rise. They moaned and screamed. They couldn't be happier.

"My Cinderello…!!"
"My prince and king!!"

Sebastian, when he noticed that they were both going to cum at the same time, took the glass shoe from Jay's foot and put it close to Jay's cock. And at that moment Cinderello, that is to say, Jay, came inside his glass shoe when he noticed that Sebastian was also coming inside him. It was so much that part of the prince's rich cum spilled out of Jay's ass and fell into the glass shoe that had come off Cinderello's perfect foot at that moment. The amount of Sebastian's milk that filled the shoe was enough for Sebastian to take it and give it to his Cinderello to drink. In turn, Sebastian took the shoe full of Jay's milk from him and also drank from the glass shoe.

And in this way, the King Sebastian and his Consort King Cinderello were happily ever after.

THE END

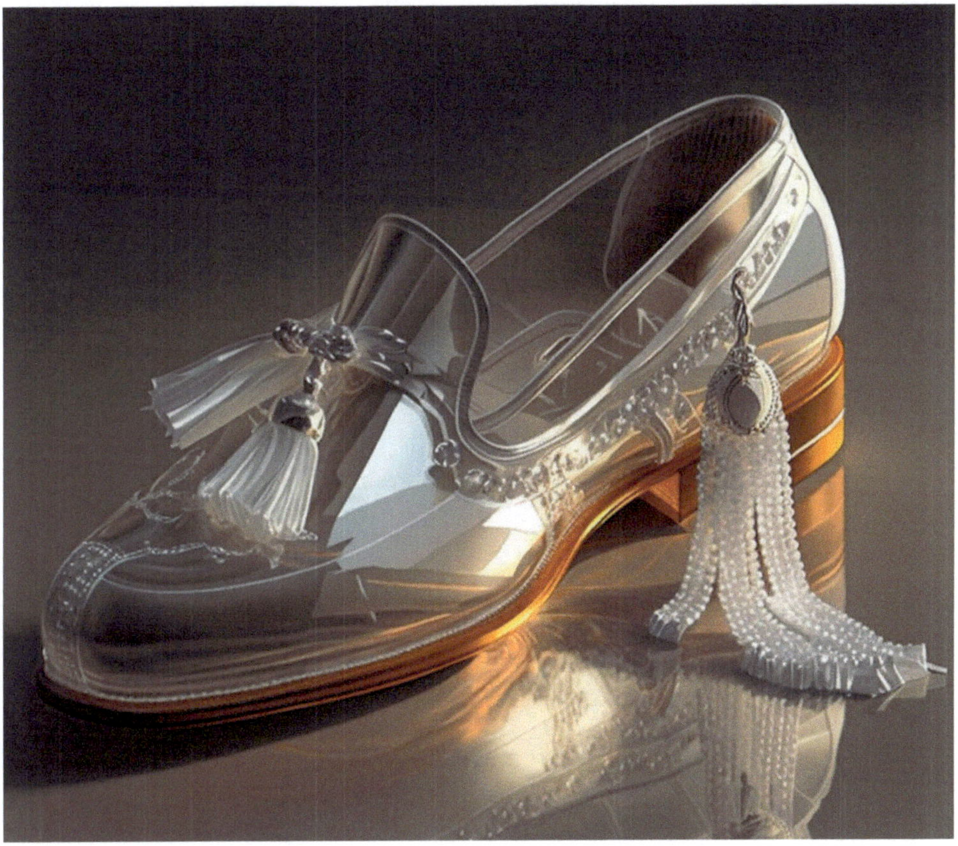

Appendix
Glass loafers Gallery

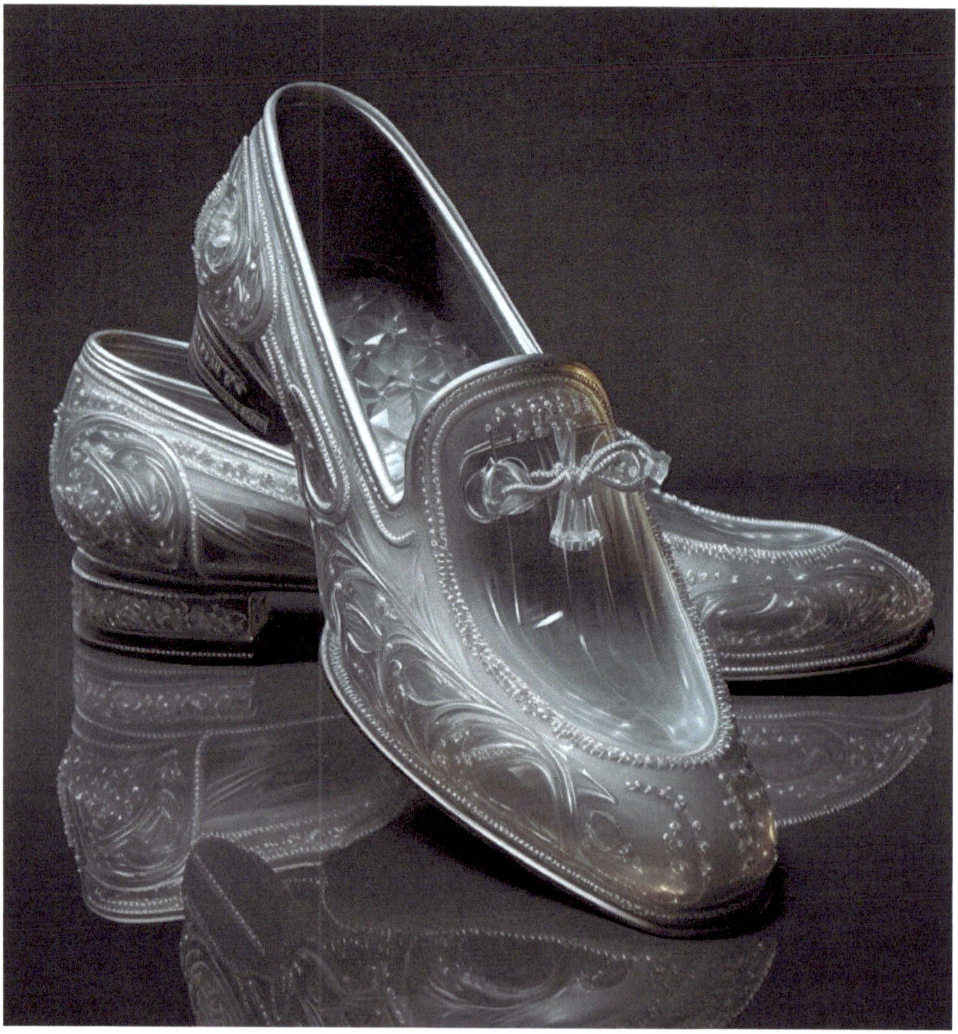

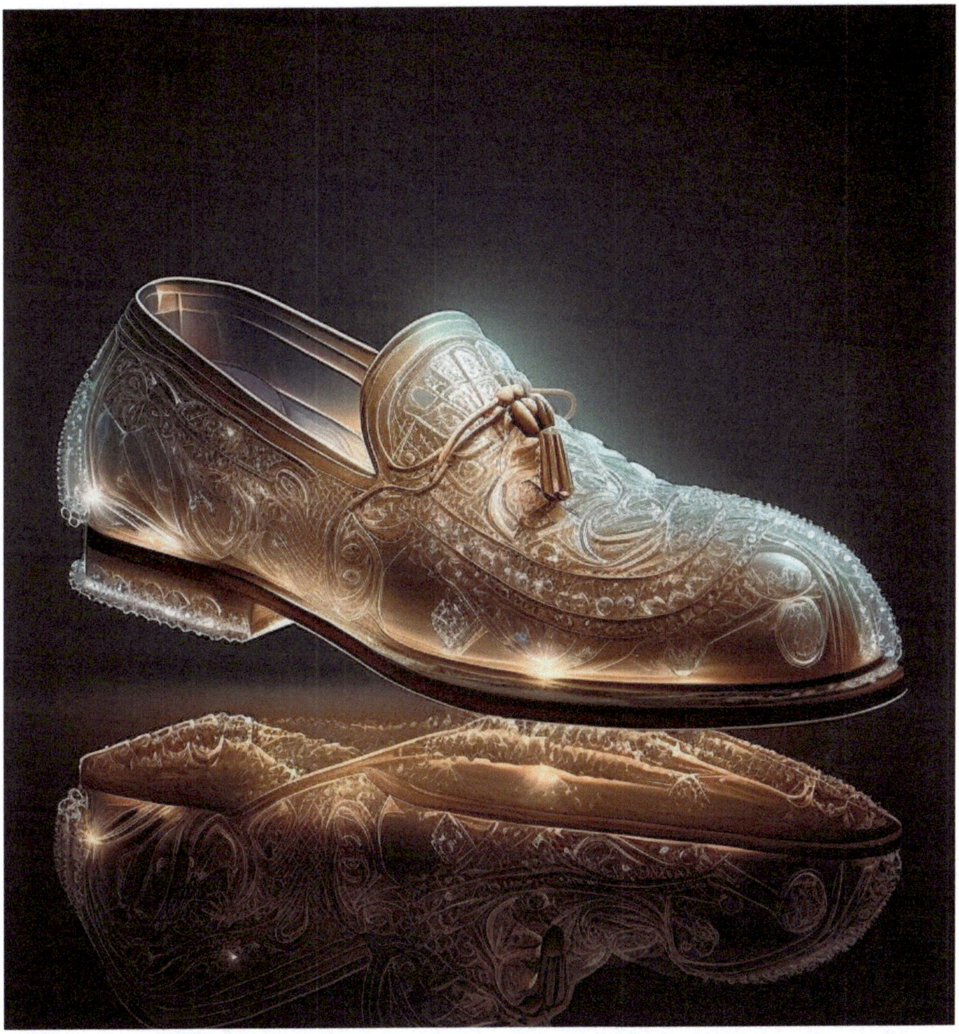

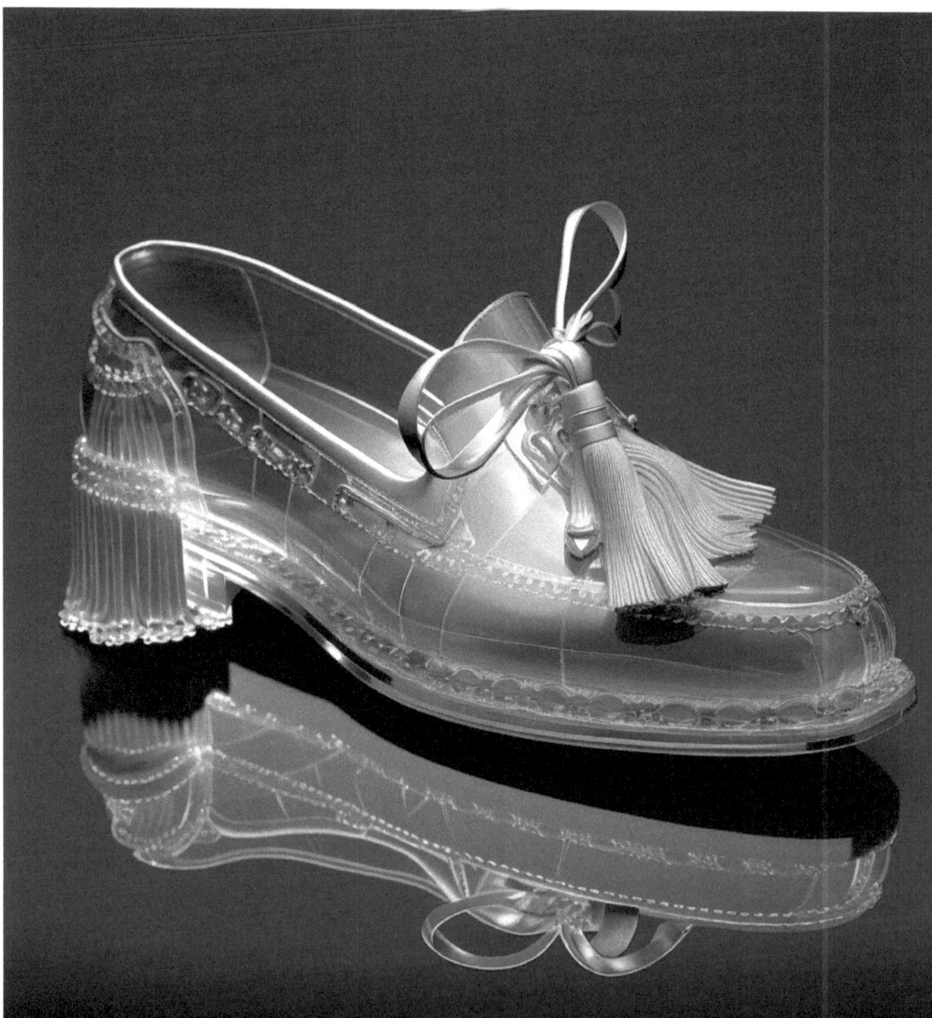

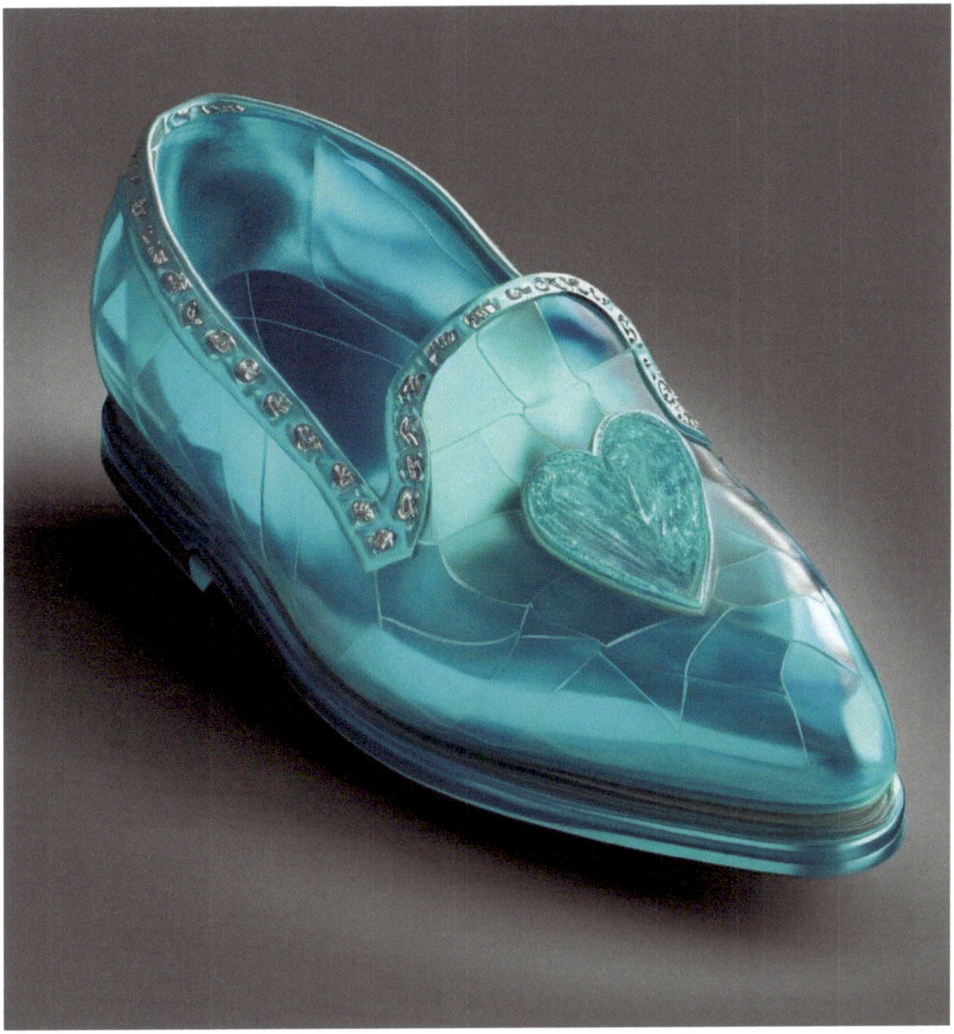

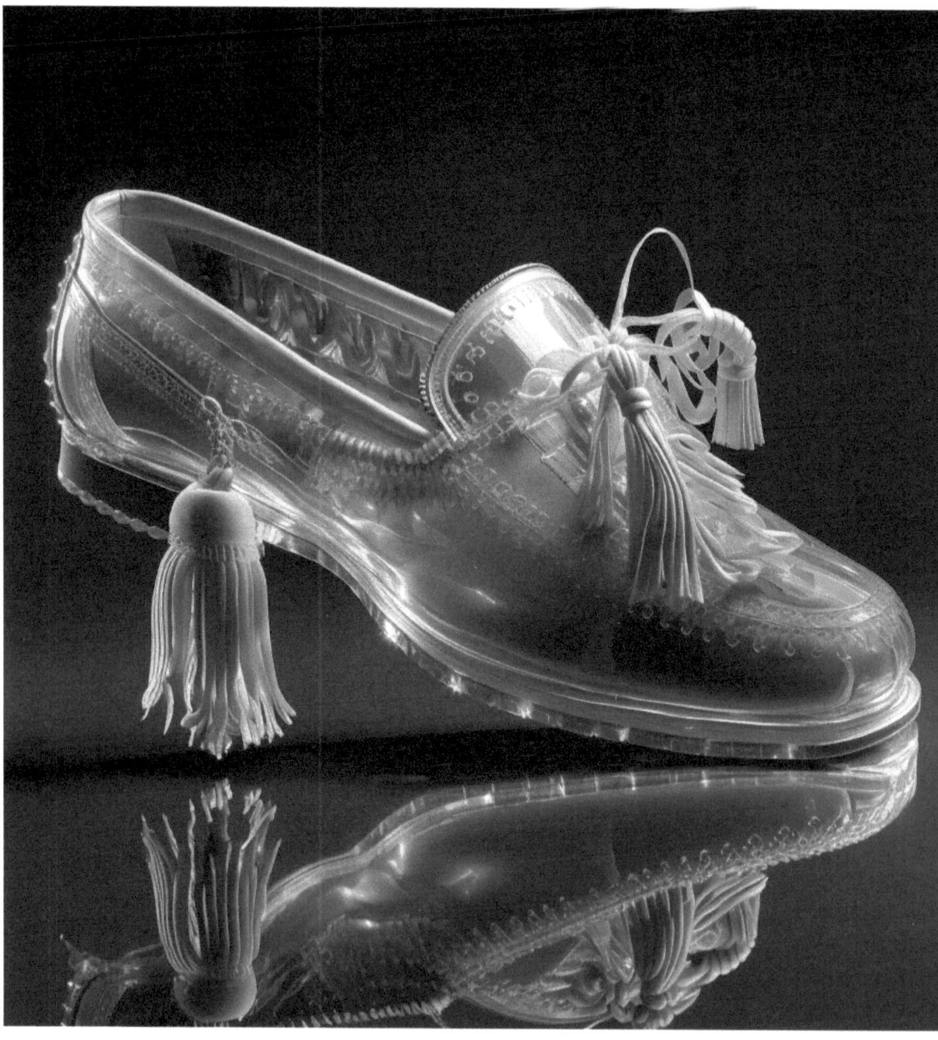

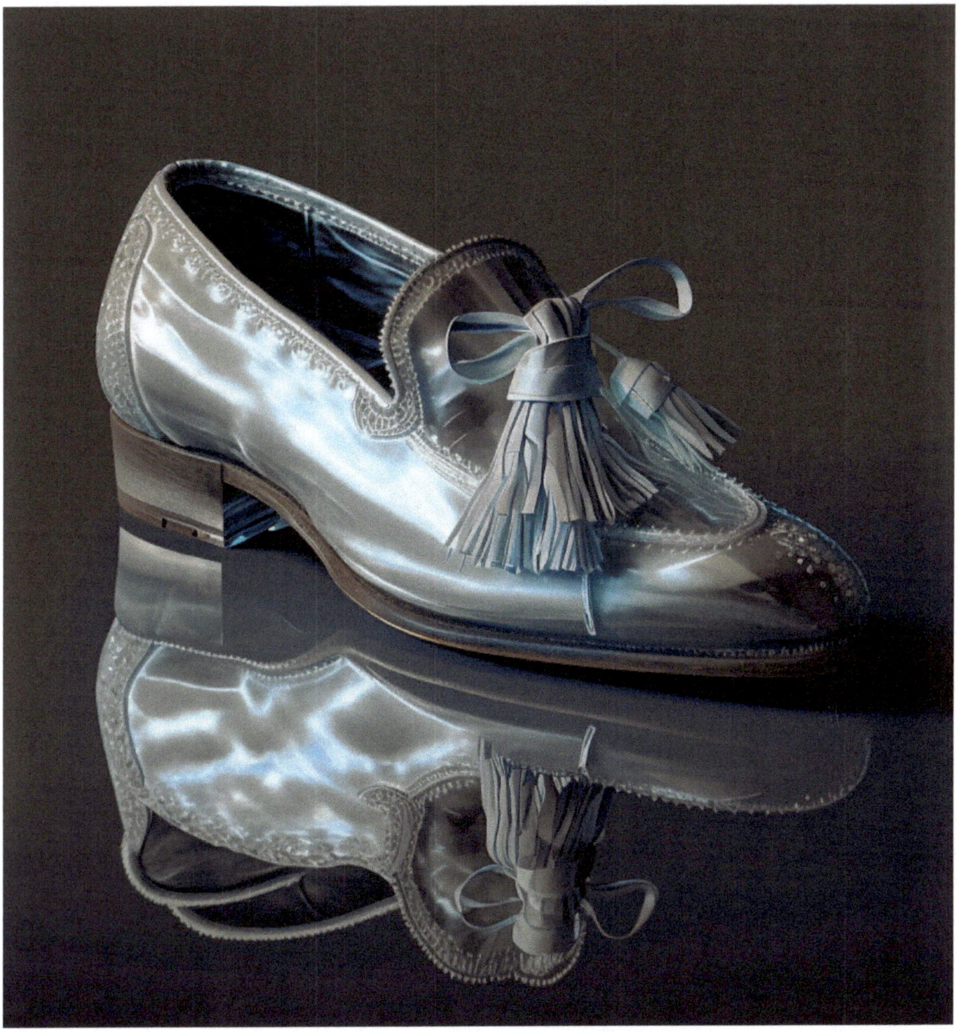

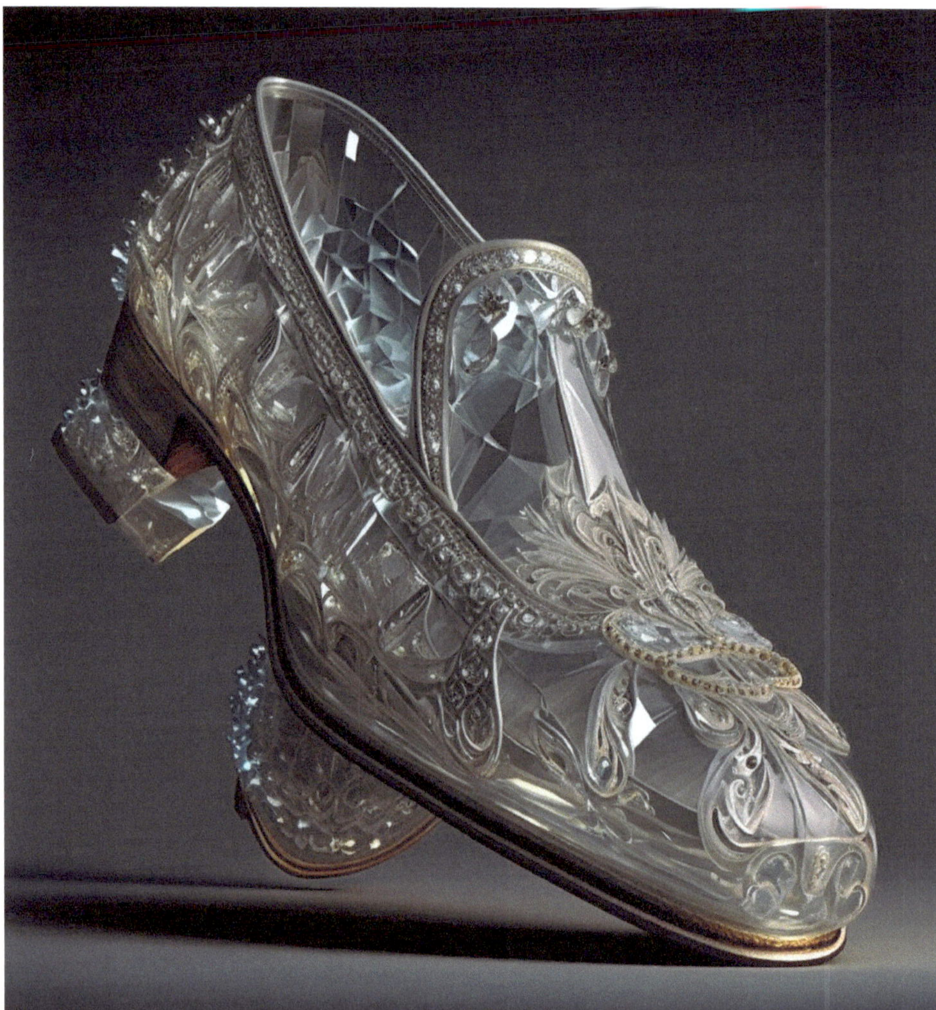

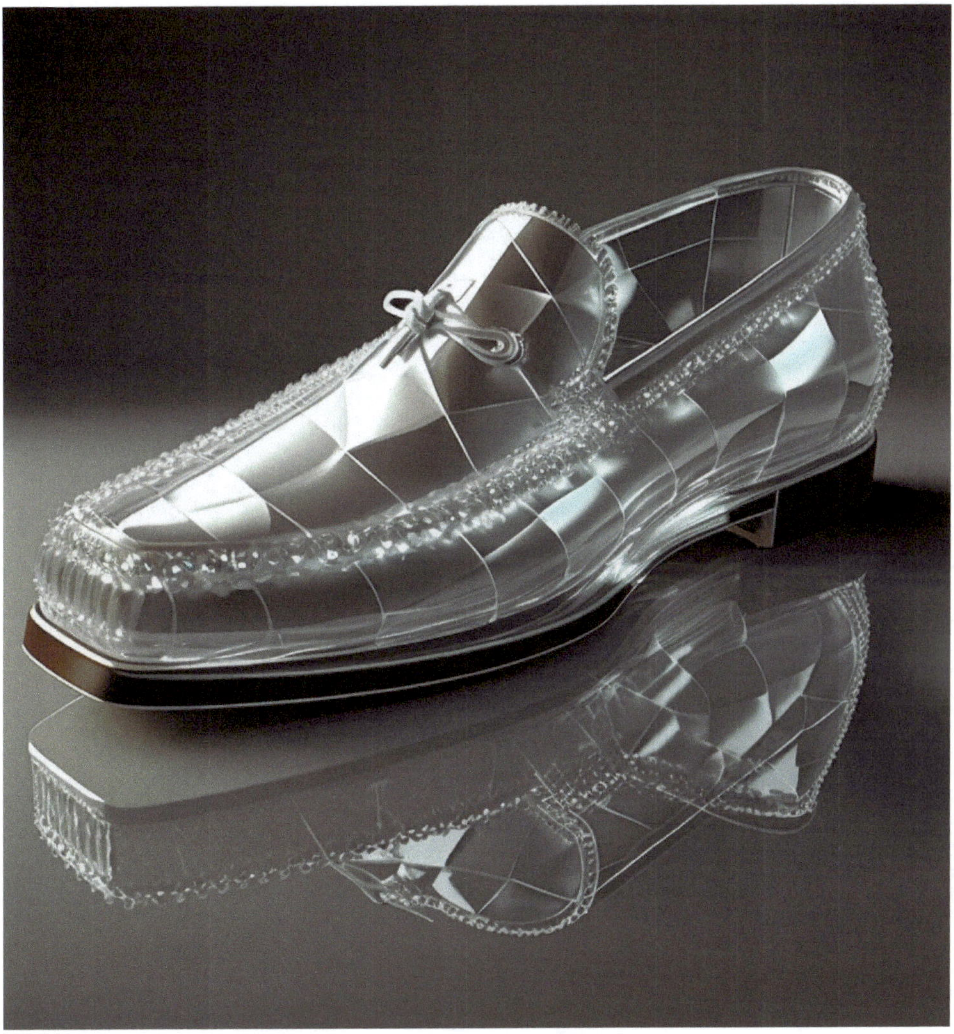

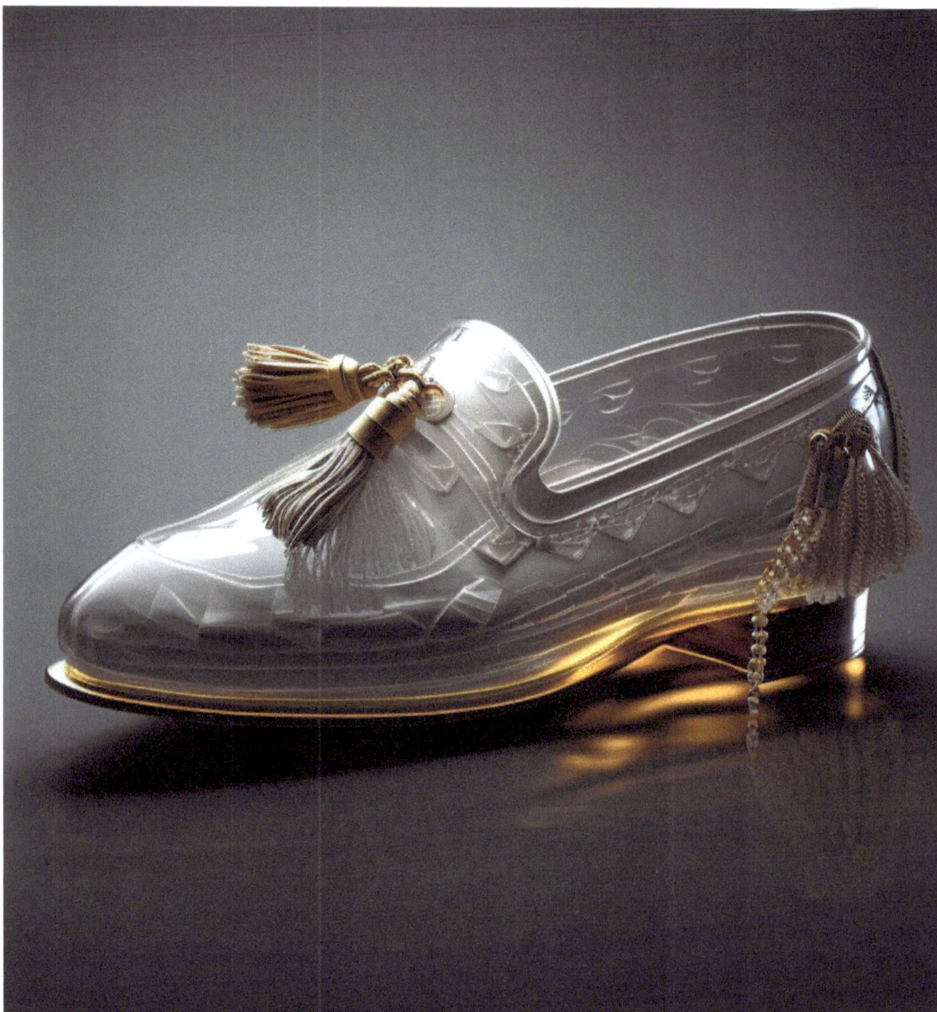

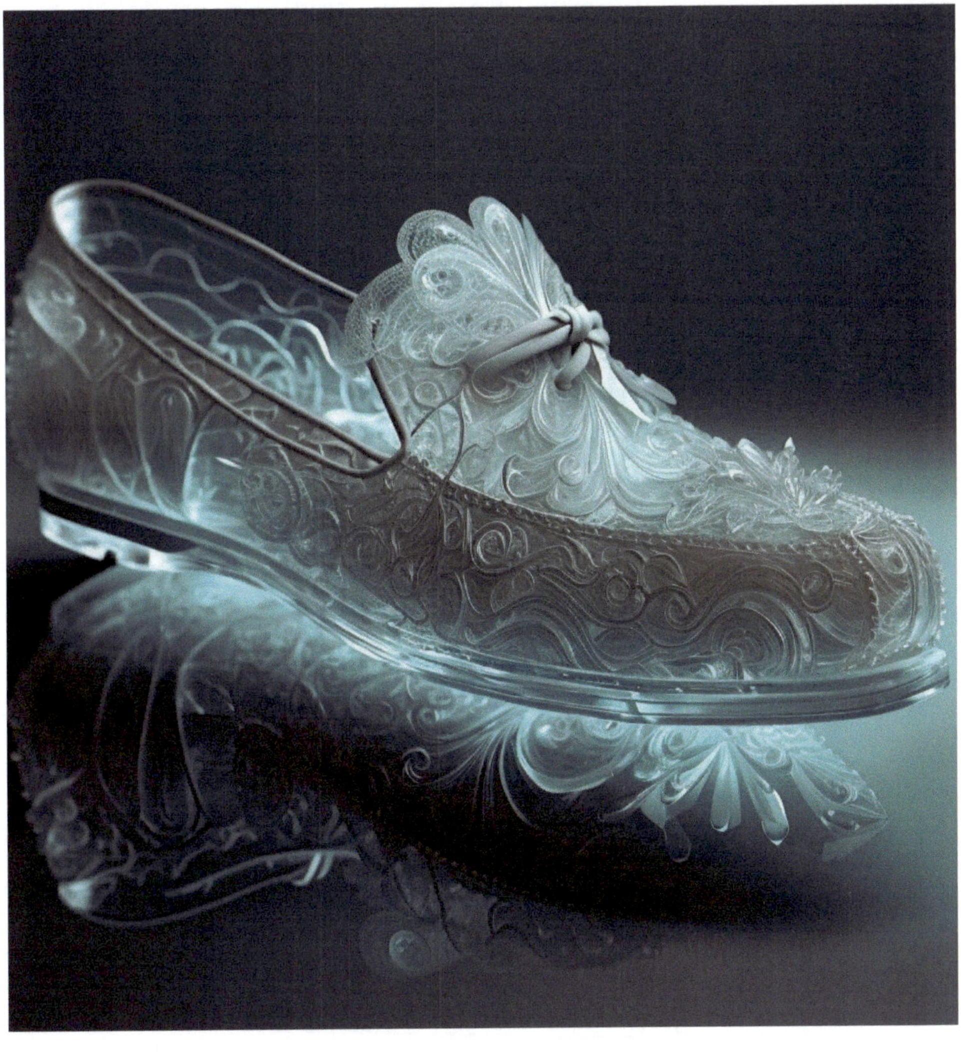

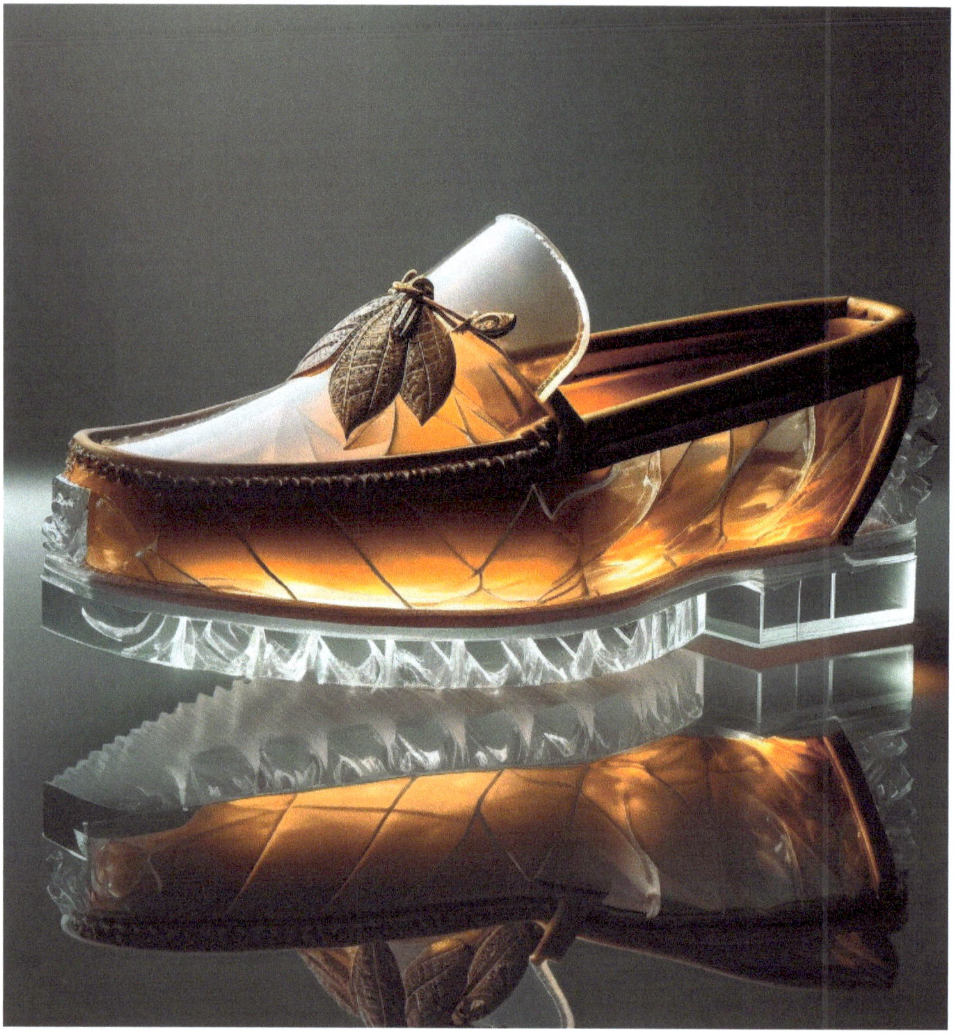

123